Raves for the Work of JACK CLARK...

"My favorite fiction novel this year was written by a taxi driver who used to hand it out to his passengers. It's a terrific story and character study...Kudos to Hard Case Crime for publishing Mr. Clark's book."
— *Quentin Tarantino*

"*Nobody's Angel* is a gem...which doesn't contain a wasted word or a false note...it's just about perfect."
— *Washington Post*

"Heartbreaking...captivating...each page turn feels like real, authentic Chicago."
— *Chicago Sun–Times*

"A pure delight for many reasons, not the least of which is the way Jack Clark celebrates and rings a few changes on the familiar private-eye script...There's a memorable moment [on] virtually every page."
— *Chicago Tribune*

"The cynical, melancholy cabbie point of view is perfect for this kind of neon-lit, noir-tinged, saxophone-scored prose poem, and Clark hits all the right notes."
— *Booklist*

"*Nobody's Angel* has the wry humor and engaging characters typical of the best of the hard-boiled genre, but Clark's portrait of Chicago in the 1990s, with its vanishing factories and jobs, its lethal public housing projects, its teenage hookers climbing into vans on North Avenue, is what gives it legs."
— *Chicago Reader*

As I slowed for the light, a young girl got off a bench. She was dressed in jeans and a powder blue jacket, with her hands pushed deep in her jacket pockets to guard against the cold.

The girl did a little step and shrugged slightly, and her jacket opened just a touch.

Her breasts were small and rounded. They seemed lighter than the surrounding skin, almost yellow, I thought, but maybe that was the glow of the street lights. Her nipples were hidden just beyond the edge of the jacket and I was almost ready to pay to see them. It was that nice a tease.

She closed the jacket and I looked up, and she smiled and blew me a kiss.

She was just another whore out on the street at five in the morning. But she was still subtle enough, or fresh enough, that she was also just a kid in jeans and sneakers.

A horn sounded and I looked up to find the light green. I pulled into the left-turn lane and looked back in the mirror. A van had pulled to the curb and the girl was leaning in the passenger window, casting a lean profile in my mirror.

I waited for a car to clear, then made the turn and headed north.

Maybe if I hadn't been drinking it wouldn't have taken so long to register. As it was, I was almost a mile away before it hit me. I made a U-turn and sped back, but the van and the girl were both gone...

Nobody's
ANGEL

by **Jack Clark**

A HARD CASE CRIME NOVEL

A HARD CASE CRIME BOOK

(HCC-065-R)

First Hard Case Crime edition: February 2024

Published by

Titan Books
A division of Titan Publishing Group Ltd
144 Southwark Street
London SE1 0UP

in collaboration with Winterfall LLC

Print edition ISBN 978-1-80336-747-7
E-book ISBN 978-1-80336-748-4

Design direction by Max Phillips
www.signalfoundry.com

Typeset by Swordsmith Productions

The name "Hard Case Crime" and the Hard Case Crime logo are trademarks of Winterfall LLC. Hard Case Crime books are selected and edited by Charles Ardai.

Printed by CPI Group (UK) Ltd, Croydon CR0 4YY

Visit us on the web at www.HardCaseCrime.com

To the memory of Mayor Harold Washington,
the best friend Chicago cabdrivers ever had.

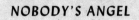

NOBODY'S ANGEL

SKY BLUE TAXI

INITIAL CHARGE	$1.20
FIRST 1/5th MILE	.20
EACH ADDITIONAL 1/6th MILE	.20
WAITING TIME (EACH MINUTE)	.20
ADDITIONAL PASSENGERS (EACH)	.50
TRUNKS	.50
HAND BAGGAGE CARRIED FREE	

(RATES IN EFFECT FROM MARCH 1990 TO JANUARY 1993)

CITY OF CHICAGO

INCORPORATED 4th MARCH 1837

PUBLIC PASSENGER CHAUFFEUR'S
LICENSE

EDWIN W
MILES

Department of Consumer Services

It was a beautiful winter night but everybody was home hiding from a snowstorm that would never arrive. Everybody but the cabdrivers. We were sitting around the Lincoln Avenue round-table—a group of rectangular tables and the surrounding booths in the back of the Golden Batter Pancake House—everybody bitching and moaning, which is the routine even on good nights.

Escrow Jake was into a familiar rant about TV weathermen. "When they say, 'Whatever you do, don't go outside,' what they really mean is: 'Stay home, watch TV and see how fast my ratings and my paycheck go up.'"

Jake had been a lawyer until he got disbarred for squandering escrow accounts at various racetracks. He was still a degenerate gambler but now he drove a cab to feed his habit. Only his very best friends called him Escrow to his face.

In the booth behind Jake, Tony Golden and Roy Davidson were schooling a rookie in the art of survival. Golden had grown up on the black South Side. Davidson was white, from the hills of Kentucky. But they were the best of friends. And they both loved the rookie. Everybody did.

There weren't many Americans entering the trade, and the kid was white to boot, which made him about as rare as a twenty dollar tip.

"Don't go south," Davidson warned him.

"Keep your doors locked," Golden advised. "Especially that left rear one. They love to slip in that left rear door."

"Don't go west," Davidson added.

"Then they can sit right behind you and when the time comes, bam, they're over the seat."

"Don't go into the projects."

"I don't even know where all the projects are." The rookie sounded shaky.

"You know what Cabrini looks like?" Davidson asked.

The rookie said he did. Everybody knew what the Cabrini-Green housing project looked like.

"That's all you got to know. Don't go south. Don't go west. Don't go anywhere looks like Cabrini."

"But I won't know till I get there," the rookie said.

Good point, kid, I thought. Good point. And I remembered my own days as a rookie and my first trip to the pancake house.

I'd cut off another taxi. The cab came around me at the next red light, pulled into the intersection, then backed right to my bumper.

The guy who'd gotten out wasn't that big, but he walked back slowly, with plenty of confidence, ignoring the horns that started to blare as the light turned green.

"Jesus, you're white," Polack Lenny said as cars squealed around us. "Why you driving like a fucking dot-head?" I was to discover that this was Lenny's harshest insult.

"Sorry. I didn't see you," I lied. "Just trying to get back to O'Hare."

"Oh, boy. How long you been driving?"

"Couple months," I admitted.

"Never go back," he said. "Haven't you learned that yet? You never go back."

"It's really moving out there," I said.

He shook his head sadly. "Stop by the Golden Batter on Lincoln some night. You can buy me a cup of coffee."

He jogged back to his cab, jumped in, and made the light as

it was changing. I waited for the next one, then wasted twenty minutes speeding to O'Hare to find the staging area full of empty cabs.

Later that night I bought Lenny a cup of coffee. It was the first of a few thousand conversations we would have at the roundtable. It was easy to learn when Lenny was talking. "People don't want to hear how bad business is," he told me that first night. "They got problems of their own. So if they ask, just lie and say you're having a great time. You might even start to believe it."

Tonight, drivers were remembering and concocting long trips. St. Louis, Louisville, Miami, Los Angeles, Anchorage. Lenny, sitting at the head of table number one, cut everybody off. "You want to talk about long trips, I'll tell you about a long trip."

Ace, sitting across from me, winked.

"Here we go," I whispered.

But the whole place shut up. There must have been thirty drivers, and many had already heard Lenny's favorite story. I'd heard it several times myself. But this is the night I always remember.

"This is years ago," Lenny said. "I'm on LaSalle Street in the Loop when this guy in a bowler hat flags me with his cane. 'Buckingham Palace, please.' Like it's right 'round the corner. 'Listen, pal,' I tell him. 'I can get you to the fountain for a couple of bucks but the palace is about four thousand miles.' 'The palace, please.' Well, I'm getting a little annoyed. 'You think I got wings?' "

Lenny does the English guy with puckered lips: " 'I believe there's a ship leaving the Port of New York in seventeen hours, twelve minutes.' So, what the hell, I get on the horn and dispatch comes back with an even twelve grand. 'Get the money up front and save the receipts.' "

"Twelve thousand dollars?" the rookie whispered as Lenny began to reel in the line.

"The English guy opens his briefcase and counts out twelve thousand in hundred dollar bills. Then he says, 'Drive on, Leonard.' "

Leonard. Half the room died. It was a brand new touch.

"Six days later we pull up in front of Buckingham Palace and he says, 'Ta-ta, Leonard. Thank you very much.' And he hands me a ten pound tip."

"Lenny, you are so full of shit," someone said, and someone else said, "You're just figuring that out?"

Didn't faze Lenny. "Hear me out. You ain't heard the kicker. So I start back for the docks. Haven't gone two blocks when all a sudden I hear, 'Sky Blue! Sky Blue!' I stop and here's this guy lugging a couple of guitars and a suitcase. 'You're a Sky Blue Cab from Chicago, right?' 'What's it look like, pal?' 'Can you take me back there? I was just on the way to the airport but I hate to fly.' 'Well, sure. But, look, it's twelve grand and I gotta have it up front. Cash.' 'That's no problem,' he says. 'Can you get me there by Saturday night? I got to be at 43rd and King Drive by six o'clock.' "

Lenny held up his hand like a cop stopping traffic. " 'Whoa. Look. Sorry, pal, nothing personal but...' " He gave it a long beat. "...'I don't go south.' "

The place exploded in laughter. Even guys who'd heard it before were howling. I looked over and the rookie was laughing along with the crowd but you could tell he didn't really get it. He was probably thinking about driving a truck for a living or something sensible like that.

Clair, my favorite waitress, came by with a coffee pot and a rag to clean up the spills. She caught my eye and flashed a smile.

Ace winked. "She likes you, Eddie."

"She's married."

"And?"

"And she's not that kind of girl," I said. But in my dreams she was.

"The things you don't know about women," Ace said.

It was another quiet night—the tail end of that same winter— the last time I saw Lenny.

I was northbound on Lake Shore Drive, fifteen over the special winter speed limit, which was supposed to keep the road salt spray from killing the saplings shivering in the median.

The lake was a vast darkness on the right. To the left lay the park and beyond that a string of high-rent highrises climbed straight into the clouds.

A shiny Mercedes shot past in the left lane. A rusty Buick followed along. I flipped the wipers on to clear the mist that had risen off the road.

A horn sounded. I looked over as a brand new cab slipped up the Belmont Avenue ramp. I slowed down a bit and the cab pulled alongside. The inside light went on and Polack Lenny pointed a long finger at his own forehead. I couldn't read his lips but I knew that he was once again calling me a dot-head. "Hey, Lenny." I turned my own light on and gave him the finger in return.

For most of the years I'd known him, we'd both driven company cabs. I hadn't known his real name until he'd won a taxi medallion in a lottery and put his own cab on the street. I'd been one of the losers in that same lottery, and I was still driving for Sky Blue Cab.

LEONARD SMIGELKOWSKI TAXI, Lenny's rear door proudly proclaimed. His last name took up the entire width of the door, which had some obvious advantages. He might never get another complaint. Everybody'd get too bogged down with the spelling.

Lenny took both hands off the steering wheel and waved them around for me to see. I could almost hear his gravelly voice, "Look, Ma, no hands." He was obviously having a good time and he was probably rubbing it in a little. I was driving a three-year-old beater with 237,000 miles on it. If I took my hands off the wheel I'd end up bathing with the zebra mussels, and Lenny knew it.

He put one hand back on the wheel and turned the other thumb down. I pointed a thumb in the same direction. It had been that kind of night. I held an imaginary cup of coffee to my lips and took a sip. Lenny shook his head, then laid his head on a pillow he made with one hand. He waved one last time, then his inside light went out and his cab dropped back.

"What was all that?" my passenger asked as I sped back to 55.

"Just your typical bitching and moaning," I explained.

"It must be kind of scary."

"What's that?"

"All those drivers."

"What drivers?"

"The ones getting shot. It must be kind of weird."

I'll bet, I thought, and I glanced in the mirror. He was slouched in the corner of the seat, looking towards the lake. His face had lost some battle years ago and was now dotted with scores of tiny craters. His hair was long and streaked with grey. He was too old to be dressed in trendy black, to be nightclubbing on a quiet Tuesday night. He was the kind of guy who would always go home alone.

"What's your line?" I asked.

"I don't follow you."

"What sort of work you do?"

"Graphic design."

"Now that sounds scary."

He laughed. "Yeah, but nobody shoots us."

"Probably all shoot yourselves out of boredom," I said.

"Hey, what's the problem, man?" The guy sat up straight and gave me a hard look.

"Just making conversation," I said, the most easygoing guy in the world.

I took the Drive until it ended, then followed Hollywood into Ridge. Past Clark Street, Ridge narrows and winds along, following some old trail. A few blocks later, parked cabs lined both curbs. Lenny wasn't the only one who'd given up early.

A skinny guy with a beaded seat cushion under his arm was leaning against one of the taxis. He looked my way and drew a circle in the air. A nothing night, I deciphered the code. I waved and tapped the horn as I passed.

The meter was at $12.80 when I stopped just shy of the Evanston line. The guy handed me a ten and three singles and got out without a word.

"Thanks, pal. I'll buy the kid a shoelace."

Everybody wants a driver who speaks English until you actually say something.

A few years earlier I would have cruised Rogers Park looking for a load. It had been one of Chicago's great cab neighborhoods. There'd always been somebody heading downtown.

There were still plenty of decent folks around, black and white, but just to be on the safe side, I turned my toplight off, flipped my NOT FOR HIRE sign down and double-checked the door locks.

The sign didn't necessarily mean what it said, and the decent folks usually knew to wave anyway. But with the sign down, I could pass the riff-raff by without worrying about complaints.

I drifted east, working my way to Sheridan Road, and then headed south back towards the city.

On Broadway, I spotted Tony Golden locking up his Checker. I tapped the horn. He looked my way and pointed both thumbs straight down.

A few minutes later, in the heart of Uptown, a couple staggered out from beneath the marquee of a boarded-up theater. I slowed to look them over, then stopped.

The woman opened the door behind me. Her blouse was undone. Someone had been in a big hurry and popped all the buttons. She'd tucked the tail into her skirt, but when she leaned into the cab, I had a clear view of some very inviting cleavage.

"Hello," I said.

"You go Gary?" she asked. She didn't sound like she'd been in country too long. She was small and dark, with high cheekbones and probably more than a trace of Indian blood. One tiny brown hand rested on the back of my seat.

"Indiana?" I asked.

She nodded and her breath reached me and suddenly she wasn't pretty at all.

"Sure," I said. Gary was thirty miles. I pushed a button to lower the driver's window and took a deep breath of city air.

"How much dollars?" she wanted to know.

"Say forty bucks." I gave her the slow-night discount. "But I gotta have the money up front." And I would have to keep the window cracked all the way.

She turned to her partner and spoke in Spanish. He was a sawed-off guy wearing cowboy boots that still left him well below average height. He pushed her out of the way and leaned in the door. His breath wasn't any better. He could barely stand. "Fucking thief," he said, and slammed the door.

I coasted a few feet then sat waiting for the light to change. In the mirror I watched the pair stumble up the block to a big, beat-up Oldsmobile, a gas guzzler if there ever was one. They were a couple of drunks left over from some after-work saloon and now little man was going to drive the lady all-the-way-the-hell to Indiana. When they got there, their breath would mix nicely with Gary's coke-furnace air.

The light changed and I started to roll.

"Cab!"

Two guys in business suits bolted out of a nearby nightclub. I stopped halfway into the intersection. A car trapped behind me blasted its horn.

The first one in the door was a kid of about thirty. He was lean and trim with short, sandy hair. He wore a pale pinstripe suit. Some sort of junior executive, I decided. The second guy looked more like the genuine article. He was ten or fifteen years older and somewhat heavier, with lines in his face and grey in his hair. His suit was a deep, dark blue with tight, gold stripes.

"Jesus Christ, get us the fuck out of this neighborhood," Junior said.

The trapped car finally got around me. "Asshole!" somebody shouted as it squealed past.

"Hey, this is a good neighborhood," I said. I followed Broadway as it curved east and went under the elevated tracks. Off to the right a group of winos were passing a bottle around. They hadn't even bothered with the time-honored paper bag.

"Looks like New York to me," Senior decided.

"You want to see some bad neighborhoods," I offered. "I'll show you some bad neighborhoods."

"I've seen enough," Senior said. "Take us back to the Hilton."

I cut over Wilson Avenue and headed towards Lake Shore Drive, a few blocks away.

"Sorry about tonight," Senior said. "Tomorrow we'll try Rush Street. Can't go wrong there."

"I'll never trust you again."

"Used to be everything north was nice. 'cept for Cabrini, of course."

"What's Cabrini?" Junior wanted to know.

"Worst housing projects in Chicago," Senior said. "You know the first trip I ever made here I got some advice that served me well. Guy told me two things to remember about Chicago. Don't go too far south and keep away from Cabrini-Green."

"Here's how it really goes," I chimed in. "Don't go too far south. Don't go anywhere west. Be careful when you go north."

"What about east?" Junior wanted to know.

We were southbound on the Drive by then. I gestured towards the lake where a light fog was rolling in. "Can you swim?"

"It's still a great city," Senior said. "Too bad we can't see anything. Best skyline in the world."

There was a wall of fog-shrouded residential highrises on our right, most of the windows dark for the night. The towers of downtown were concealed behind thick clouds.

"Where you guys from?" I asked.

"Indy."

"Naptown," I said.

"A nice place to raise a family," the senior man informed me.

"We've got some of those around here someplace," I remembered.

An empty Yellow shot past, its toplight blazing away.

"I hear you guys been having some problems," Senior said as I flipped the wipers on in the taxi's wake.

"What's that?"

"Somebody killing cabdrivers."

"Christ." That was all anybody wanted to talk about.

"Seven guys killed, that's something."

"Three," I corrected him.

"Seven, three, whatever," Senior said. "It's gotta make you nervous."

"I've been driving for twenty years," I lied, "I was born nervous."

They both laughed.

"You know what a taxi rolling through the ghetto is?" I asked.

"What's that?"

"An ATM on wheels."

"You don't go there, do you?" Junior said.

"Where?"

"You know, those neighborhoods."

"I don't have any choice."

"Just pass 'em by," Senior advised.

"It isn't that easy," I explained. "Say you're driving by some fancy highrise and the doorman steps out blowing his whistle. You pull in and out walks the maid going home. What you gonna do?"

"Just step on the gas," Junior had the answer.

"Then they write your number down and call the Vehicle man."

"Yeah, but you're alive," Senior said.

"But eventually I'm out of a job. And, what's the big deal? It's just some old lady trying to get home."

"And you'll just be another dead cabdriver," Senior said.

"There's worse things."

"Name some."

"What kind of work you guys do?"

"Sales," Senior answered.

"Hardware." Junior fell into the trap.

"There you go." I said.

It took a minute to sink in. "They must send you people to school, teach you to be so disagreeable," Senior said.

"Just something I learned from all my wonderful passengers." And that was the end of that conversation.

I got off at Wacker Drive and took the lower level around the basements of the Loop. This was the city's famous two-level street. The downstairs was dark and dingy, full of loading docks, dumpsters, rats and bums. The detour added about a mile to the trip. The Hardy Boys knew what I was doing but neither had the balls to call me on it.

"Fourteen-fifty," I said when we pulled up in front of the Hilton.

Hotel Steve's Yellow was in the cab stand. Steve appeared to be sound asleep. But he'd wake at the first sign of a suitcase. "The ritzier the hotel," he'd told me once, "the worse the tip." And he was the man who would know. He spent a good part of his life asleep in hotel lines.

Senior threw a twenty over the front seat. "Keep the change, asshole," he said. I guess he was trying to prove some point but it was lost on me. I wouldn't have tipped myself a dime.

I cruised downtown for a while but nothing was going on. Traffic signals turned from red to green to amber. Three out of four cars were empty cabs.

The cleaning ladies were getting off work, hurrying towards State Street to get the bus out to the Southwest Side. The last time one took a taxi was 1947.

I drove up Dearborn, beating a Checker for the federal courthouse side of the street, then cruised along hoping for a lawyer or maybe a late-night jury but there was nobody around.

At Monroe, two guards led a bum up from the First National Bank plaza and pointed him south.

Up the street, the Picasso sculpture rusted away in the plaza of the Daley Center. Nobody came up from the subway. A Flash Cab cut in front of me and turned west. I continued north, over the river.

Empty cabs were sitting in front of most of the popular nightclubs. More sleeping drivers, a sure sign they'd been waiting too long.

In an industrial area north of Chicago Avenue, I pulled into an alley to take a leak. A van was sitting in darkness at the other end of the alley. I started to back out to find a more secluded spot but then the lights of the van came on and it pulled away. I shifted back into drive, coasted to the middle of the alley, stopped, turned my headlights off and opened the door.

There was a truck yard on my side of the alley, enclosed by a cyclone fence which was strewn with windblown litter and overgrown weeds. On the other side of the alley an old factory had been converted to lofts.

I was almost finished when I heard the sound. It was muted at first, a cat's cry floating on the wind. Then it came again, louder and much closer, a strange, high-pitched whimper. The hairs on the back of my neck stood on edge. I finished quickly, jumped in the cab and stepped on the gas.

Toward the end of the alley where the van had been, a pile of garbage lay across my path. As I approached, the pile shifted. Something flashed briefly, caught in the headlight beam. A pair of eyes.

I heard my father's voice, my very first driving lesson: "Never run over a pile of leaves." I laid on the brakes, jammed the cab into reverse, and shot back out the way I'd come in.

I sat there facing the alley. I flashed my brights a few times but now there was nothing to see; just a dark pile alongside an overflowing dumpster. Could I have imagined the eyes?

I turned east and started away. Whatever or whoever it was, it wasn't my concern.

That got me out to Wells Street, where a string of empty cabs was heading north for home. I didn't see anybody I knew. That's the way the business was heading, more Indian, Pakistani, and East African drivers and fewer Americans every day.

I thought about the eyes, about the movement in the pile of trash. It was probably nothing, I decided. And I remembered Polack Lenny's lesson: Never go back.

Oh, the hell with that. I released the brake, circled the block and pulled up to the mouth of the alley, about ten feet shy of the dumpster. I stopped with my headlights trained on the pile, grabbed my canister of mace, got out and approached slowly.

There was a rolled-up furniture pad lying next to the dumpster. The pad was torn and soiled and, if there was anything inside, it wasn't very big. I tiptoed closer and there weren't any eyes. There was broken glass scattered around—maybe some of that had reflected my headlight beam. "Hello," I said, just to be sure, and I tapped the pad with my foot.

The pad moved. I jumped back as a corner slid downwards and the pair of eyes reappeared. They didn't look up. They were just there. A pair of shadowy eyes set in a small dark face.

I moved forward slowly, holding the mace out front, my finger ready on the trigger. Christ, it looked like a kid. A little black kid hiding in a furniture pad in the middle of an alley. Two narrow wrists were crossed and a pair of tiny black hands gripped the edge of the pad.

It was a girl, I realized. She was lying on her side, curled up inside the pad. If size was all I had to go on, I would have guessed she was somewhere around nine or ten. But there was something much older in those eyes. "You okay?" I said.

"I'm cold, mister," she whispered. I could barely make out the words. "Real cold."

"You're gonna be okay," I said and the girl uncrossed her wrists and showed me how wrong I was.

The pad opened. Someone had cut her to ribbons. Thick brown ribbons and narrow red ones that flowed down her chest and soaked into the pad. I turned my head away. "I'll get help," I whispered and I hurried back to the cab.

I grabbed the microphone and hit the switch for the two-way radio. "Ten-thirteen," I shouted. "Ten-thirteen!"

A dispatcher came on. I gave him my location and cab number. "There's a kid here, in the alley," I said, leaning into the cab so she wouldn't hear. "I think she's been stabbed. She's bleeding real bad."

"Stand by, sir, while I call the police."

"Call an ambulance," I said.

"Check," the dispatcher said.

I looked up. The girl had rolled and now lay on her back, one knee in the air, the pad wide open. She wasn't wearing a stitch of clothes. Her chest was a bloody mess. Her head was turned my way but even in the headlight beam her eyes seemed hidden behind a cloud.

A triangular patch of curly black hair caught my attention. She was no nine year old. But she was still a kid. Fourteen or fifteen. That was my new guess. A kid that someone had dumped like a piece of garbage.

I switched my headlights off. "They're gonna get help," I called. For a second her eyes seemed to focus. "You're gonna be okay," I said.

It seemed like long minutes before the dispatcher finally

returned. "The police and ambulance are on the way," he announced.

"Thanks."

"The police request that you stay there until they arrive."

"I'm not going anywhere," I said.

"Thank you, units, for standing by," the dispatcher said, addressing the rest of the Sky Blue fleet. "At 1:07 A.M. the emergency is clear. Let's go back to work."

I flicked the radio off. "The ambulance is on the way," I said. In the distance I heard the first siren.

"I'm cold," the girl said.

I walked over and lifted one end of the pad and draped it back over her. It was heavy with blood and with pebbles and dirt that clung to it. A hand grabbed my leg. Even through my trousers it felt as cold as ice. "Don't go," the girl said softly, and then she said something too faint to hear.

I crouched down. "My angel," she whispered. Her hand reached up and found one of my hands and held it tight. "Are you Relita's angel?"

The first squad car came barreling around the corner, siren crying and blue lights flashing. I stood up slowly as the squad screeched to a halt. "You're gonna be okay," I said, and her hand slipped away.

A short heavyset black woman jumped out the driver's door of the squad. "Stay right where you are," she said, pointing a stubby finger my way. I stayed where I was while she reached back into the car and came out with a hat to match her uniform.

The other cop, a chubby white guy with pink cheeks and a baby face, approached hatless, flashlight in hand. He seemed much too young to be a cop. But he had the gun and the badge, and the flashlight, which he shone straight into my eyes.

"Come out of there slowly," the woman said.

I put my hands up to shield my eyes. "I can't see."

"Just walk straight ahead," Baby-face advised.

I walked until I reached my cab.

"That's far enough," the woman let me know. "Now put your hands on the hood. Back up a little. Spread your legs."

"You know, I'm the one called you guys."

A second squad car came screeching to a halt. I looked back under my arm. Two cops jumped out and headed for the girl.

Baby-face frisked me while the woman stood holding the light. He went all the way down to my ankles. "Okay," he said when he was done. "Why don't you tell us what happened."

I pushed off the car. A third squad car pulled into the far end of the alley. "I don't know," I started to explain.

The woman trained the light on the hood of the cab. There was blood where my hands had been.

"Turn around," Baby-face said, and I turned around to find him holding the flashlight. "Let's see your hands," he said.

I held out my hands and there was no hiding the blood. "I was holding her hand," I explained.

"Turn 'em over."

I turned my palms up.

"We're gonna stick you in the back for a minute," the woman cop decided. She walked over and opened the door of the squad car. Baby-face escorted me over.

I slid into the back seat. The woman started to close the door, then stopped. "You got a driver's license, I presume." She held out her hand. I pulled my wallet out and handed her the license. She closed the door.

I caught sight of my reflection in the shield that separated the back seat from the front. "You stupid son of a bitch," I said to it.

*

It was the social event of the night for the boys and girls in blue. One squad followed another and soon the street was a galaxy of flashing blue lights. Each new arrival had to get their fill of blood, then they would back off and stand around in small groups talking and smoking cigarettes, laughing like there wasn't any kid bleeding to death a few feet away.

The ambulance came, and suddenly there was a big production moving cars to make room for it, as if its arrival were somehow a surprise. Baby-face got in my cab and backed it out of the way.

The detectives showed up while they were loading the girl into the ambulance. She was so slight she barely made a bump on the stretcher. How old was she really, I wondered. Without warning, an image of my daughter slipped into my mind.

I tried to push it away by concentrating on the scene outside. There were two detectives. One was tall and very distinguished looking. He might have been a senator. He had thick, snow white hair and wore a grey trench coat. He looked tanned and relaxed, like he'd just gotten back from a Florida vacation.

The younger detective was even taller but extremely thin. He pulled out a slender notebook and began to write.

The woman cop walked up and started to wave her arms around. She pointed my way and the detectives looked over. The senator lit a cigarette, took a few quick drags, then tossed it away and climbed into the ambulance. The younger detective continued to write.

I looked down at the wallet in my hands, opened the back compartment. The smiling face, protected by plastic, stared back.

The photo had been taken by a street photographer at Buckingham Fountain one summer Sunday. She'd been eight years old back then. A little girl whose blond hair was beginning to turn brown, standing with her father, a tower of water rising behind us.

My complexion was naturally dark and I could usually pass for Greek or Italian or any of the other Mediterranean lines. But in the photograph my skin appeared bleached. I'd lost way too much weight and it wasn't from dieting. I was unshaven, disheveled, obviously hung over. It had been the worst year of my life. But my daughter didn't see any of that. She was smiling up at me with such obvious love and devotion that seven years after the lens had snapped shut, the photograph still broke my heart. I only saw her one more time. That was her reward for all that love.

She would be fifteen now, out in sunny California with my ex-wife and her new husband.

For years, I'd been waiting for the phone to ring or for a letter to arrive or, dream of dreams, to find her sitting on my doorstep.

The door of the squad car opened. "You ready to come out of there, Edwin?"

I looked up as the ambulance pulled away. The detectives stood waiting.

"Eddie," I said.

"Eddie it is," the senator said. "I'm Hagarty. This is Detective Foster."

"How you doing?" I asked as I got out of the car.

"Hold out your hands," Foster said.

I held out my hands and then turned them over as they examined them under a flashlight beam.

"I was holding her hand," I said.

"Tell us what happened," Hagarty said.

"I don't know," I said, as Foster shone the light down my shirt and pants. "I just found her."

"How did that happen?" Hagarty asked.

"I stopped to take a leak," I said. "When I was pulling out I saw her. I mean, I didn't know what it was but it was moving. So I backed out and came around the block."

"Did she say anything?" Hagarty asked as Foster pulled out a camera and started snapping pictures.

"Just that she was cold."

"Anything else?"

I shook my head, then held out my hands as Foster moved in for a close-up.

He put the camera away and took my arm. "Why don't you show us where you took this piss."

I led them past my cab which had all the doors and the trunk open, and down the alley. "Somewhere 'round here," I said.

Foster shone the light around. There were several patches of wet pavement and a large puddle from a recent rain. "What do you think?" he asked.

"Too much coffee," Hagarty said. He pulled out a penlight and aimed it at a bunch of weeds growing along the fence. "Queen Anne's Lace," he said.

Foster swung his own light that way. "Well, well, well," he said.

"You see anybody else around?" Hagarty asked.

I told them about the van.

"What kind of van?"

"I don't know," I said. "Just a van."

"You can do better than that," Hagarty said.

I closed my eyes and tried. "It was brown or maybe red," I decided after a moment. "Could have been a Ford. I'm not sure."

"Don't stop now," Hagarty said as Foster scribbled away in his notebook.

"It had a ladder on the back," I remembered. "You know, so you can climb up to the roof. That's all I remember."

"Was there a spare tire back there?" Hagarty asked.

"I don't remember."

"Tear drop windows?"

"Huh?"

"You know one of those customized jobs."

"Sorry," I shrugged.

"Illinois plates?"

"I don't know."

We walked out of the alley and stopped alongside the cab. "There was a bumper sticker on the back," I remembered one last thing. "I don't know what it said but it was yellow with dark letters."

Foster scribbled some more in the notebook, then pulled my driver's and chauffeur's licenses out of a coat pocket. "This your right address?"

"Yeah."

"How about a phone number?"

I gave him my phone number.

"What's your sheet look like?"

"Huh?"

"Do you have a record?" Hagarty translated.

"Just some stuff with my ex-wife," I said.

"Like what?" Foster asked.

"Domestic battery," I said. "It was all bullshit. She got a restraining order, the whole bit."

"Anything else?"

I shook my head. Wasn't that enough? She'd ended up taking my daughter away.

Foster handed me my licenses. "What're you planning to do with that mace?" he asked.

"What do you think?"

"Good luck."

Hagarty lit a cigarette. Foster put his notebook away and stuck a cigarette in his mouth but didn't light it.

"Is she gonna die?" I asked.

Hagarty shrugged. "Last year we had a couple cabdrivers," he said out of the blue.

"Yeah, when they weren't getting any press," Foster said. "Now they're all over the front page and all we get is winos and whores."

"You guys need me anymore?" I asked.

"No, you can get out of here," Hagarty said, "soon as these clowns get out of your way." He handed me a business card. *Detective James Hagarty, Violent Crimes*, it read. "You remember anything, or you see that van driving around, give us a call."

Foster pulled out his notebook and scribbled one last line. He threw his cigarette away unlit then closed the notebook. I got in the cab. The contents of the glove box were scattered over the front seat. I started the engine and turned on the lights. The two detectives got into an unmarked Chevy and pulled away.

My cab was surrounded by squad cars but the cops weren't in any hurry. They finished their stories and their cigarettes.

I gathered up the insurance card, owner's manual, the pads of receipts, matchbooks and lost disposable lighters, and crammed them back into the glove compartment, then sat there waiting, wishing I still smoked.

The girl would be in the hospital by now. They'd be putting her back together and, from what I'd seen, her odds weren't good. But for some reason I was sure she'd survive. I said a little prayer. Relita, it was such a strange name.

I turned the FM on long enough to hear a few riffs of jazz trumpet then tried the two-way radio where there was nothing but static.

I sat there listening to it, waiting.

After a while the clowns got out of my way.

The dome light when lit, must be visible at 300 feet in normal sunlight. The dome light shall be installed and maintained in such manner that the dome light will automatically be lit when the taximeter is not activated and that the dome light will automatically be unlit when the taximeter is activated.

City of Chicago, Department of Consumer Services,
Public Vehicle Operations Division

I headed north into the heart of the bar rush. The early saloons were just closing. The smart drunks were heading home, and the not-so-smart ones were moving on to the late bars which would close in two hours at 4 A.M.

But I didn't feel like ferrying drunks around. One guy gave me the finger when he realized I wasn't stopping. A girl jumped up and down and waved both arms in the air. There was a switch that turned the toplight off but I left it burning.

I turned northwest up Lincoln Avenue. There wasn't a single cab in front of the Golden Batter Pancake House, the home of the Lincoln Avenue Roundtable. Everybody had gone home. I continued past to Cut-Rate Gas.

There were several cabs at the pumps. A group of drivers was standing around watching another driver clean the windows of his cab. I didn't know any of them. I parked at the farthest pump. The drivers were all jabbering away in their native tongue.

I started the pump then walked inside. I waved to the kid behind the counter—he was half hidden by dangling instant lottery tickets—then headed to the washroom.

My hands were sticky with blood. I turned the water on and let it run awhile but it barely got lukewarm. I added some soap and washed the stains away.

While I was waiting for my change, the early edition of the *Sun-Times* caught my eye. "SIX KILLED IN NIGHT OF VIO-LENCE," the headline screamed. "12-Year-Old & Cabdriver Are Victims," a smaller headline read.

I picked up a copy and skimmed straight to the cabdriver. "Abdul Patel, 41, a driver for North Suburban Taxi, was found stabbed to death in Garfield Park on the city's West Side. His abandoned taxi was found several hours later in an alley a few blocks west of the park. Investigators believe Patel was killed in his cab then his body dumped in the park.

"Police are checking cab company records in an attempt to determine where Patel picked up his last passenger.

"Three Chicago cabdrivers have been slain in the city so far this year. Patel is the first suburban driver to be killed. He is survived by his wife and two children."

I dropped the paper back on the pile. "Anybody you know?" the kid behind the counter said.

"Some suburban driver," I said. "What the hell was he doing on the West Side?"

The kid shrugged. How would he know?

I pushed through the door, popped the trunk, grabbed a handful of paper towels and a bottle of window cleaner. I cleaned the steering wheel and wiped the blood off the hood, then climbed into the back seat and started my usual end-of-shift cleanup.

When I crawled out, one of the foreign drivers was waiting. He was about five foot two, dressed in a suit and tie, like he worked in an office somewhere. "Hello, sir," he said in a sing-song voice. "Would you be coming to the meeting?" He handed me a single sheet of paper.

"CAB DRIVER SECURITY MEETING," it read in big bold print. "ALL DRIVERS PLEASE COME TO THE FOSTER AVENUE BEACH PARKING LOT AT 10 A.M. WEDNESDAY. WE MUST STOP THE KILLINGS!!!"

I handed it back. "I haven't been up that early in years," I said, and I started washing the windows.

The driver followed along. "It's important everyone come," he said.

"It's important I sleep."

Wherever used in these regulations, the term "cab stand" or "cab line" means a fixed area in the roadway alongside and parallel to the curb set aside by city ordinance for taxicabs to stand or wait for passengers, which stands are designated by metal signs or posts indicating stand capacity and bearing stand identification numbers; "chauffeur" means a Public Chauffeur as defined in Chapter 28.1 MCC; "commissioner" means the Commissioner of Consumer Services or his designee; "diving" means picking up or attempting to pick up passengers by by-passing a cab line or authorized airport staging area. Wherever used in these rules, the use of the masculine gender includes the feminine gender; the singular includes the plural and the plural the singular.

City of Chicago, Department of Consumer Services,
Public Vehicle Operations Division

I had an efficiency apartment off Montrose Avenue; a small living room, a tiny bedroom and a stand-up kitchen on the top floor of a large, brown-brick monstrosity named the Rosewood Arms. Most of the neighbors—those who spoke English—referred to it as the Armpit.

I'd moved in seven years before, intending to stay a few months. Now I was one of the senior residents. It was a building of long, narrow hallways. One dark door after another, each with a numbered brass knocker.

In the kitchen I poured a few ounces of Kentucky whiskey into a glass, cut it with a splash of tap water and added a single ice cube.

Once upon a time, I'd spent too many nights with a drink in

hand. Now I rarely thought of drinking, except as a waste of time and money. But then a night like this would come along and the lure of the whiskey would be irresistible. Just holding the glass in my hand, swirling the ice around the rim, seemed to relieve some tension.

I carried the glass to the living room and sat in the dark, my feet resting on the window ledge. In a while the day people would start lining up at the corner bus stop. I would hear air brakes hiss, and then a Chicago Transit Authority bus would shriek to a stop and they would all climb aboard, and the day would officially begin.

And then, full morning with the rest of the world wide awake, it would be time to pull down the shades and go to sleep.

I'd been a day person once. I'd had a good job, a house on a quiet, tree-lined street, a family. Now I usually managed to sleep through those too-bright hours.

At 5:15 the clock radio went off in Betty Cunningham's apartment. A while later, I could hear her on the other side of our common wall, getting ready for work.

When she'd moved in, three years before, we'd spent about two months as full-time lovers. But we'd been doomed from the start. She worked days, as an assembler in an electronics factory, and I drove nights, and neither one of us thought the other worth changing shifts for.

Betty was a few months older than I was, a Kentucky transplant who wore tons of makeup, chain-smoked Virginia Slims and still managed to be overweight. And, let's be honest, I wasn't any prize.

She'd had a few boyfriends since my time but none had lasted even as long as I had, so I could always console myself that I wasn't the worst of the lot.

Now, when Betty didn't have anything going on, we'd get together Sunday mornings after I got off work.

We'd usually have breakfast, and then spend some time in her bedroom. Irv, my dayman, never worked Sundays, so I had the cab all day. If it was nice we'd take a ride along the lakefront, maybe up through the North Shore to gaze at the homes of the rich. Or we'd see a movie, or have an early dinner somewhere, or just lie around napping and watching TV.

We seldom saw each other during the week. But Betty had the strange knack of knowing when I was awake in the morning. I could be sitting absolutely still at the window and she'd knock lightly at the door. But she never knocked once I was in the bedroom.

Today, I stopped in the kitchen on the way to the door and added a splash of whiskey.

Betty looked at the glass, took a whiff of the air, then a drag on her cigarette. She blew a long stream of smoke my way. I held the glass up in a toast.

"Christ, what time did you get home?" She leaned against the hallway wall.

"About three," I admitted.

"Slow night?"

I nodded.

"You should have hollered." She smiled.

I shrugged and she rewarded me with another stream of cigarette smoke.

"I really wouldn't mind sometimes." She fluttered her eyelashes and faked a blush and that was more than enough for me.

"Come on," I said, and I tried to pull her inside, but she danced away and wagged a finger at me.

"Time to catch my bus."

It was the same old story. I always wanted her when she was

right there in front of me. But I barely thought about her when she wasn't around.

Betty waved and started away, then stopped and turned back. "Eddie, there was something on the radio. They said another cabdriver…"

"Some suburban driver." I nodded. "I saw it in the paper."

"See you Sunday." She blew a final stream of smoke my way.

"Sunday," I said, and I watched her walk down the hall. She always looked great in jeans.

I went back to the window and watched her sprint for the bus. I sat there sipping the whiskey and then, hours after the bus had gone, I picked up the phone and dialed.

The line echoed back two thousand miles, then the phone began to ring. This was a call I'd been making every few months for years. I never talked to anybody. Usually an answering machine picked up. It was just a small way of keeping in touch. I sat with my finger on the cradle, ready to hang up at the sound of my ex-wife's voice.

"Hello?" a voice answered the phone. It was a younger voice, a gentle voice.

I didn't say anything.

"Hello," the voice said again, and then I was sure.

"Cookie?"

"I'm sorry," she said pleasantly. "You must have the wrong number." Cookie was a nickname I'd given her when she was two. It didn't surprise me to find that my ex-wife no longer used it.

"Laura?"

"Who's calling please?"

"Laura, it's your dad," I said.

"Daddy?" she said, and all my troubles were gone.

"Oh, baby, you don't know how I've missed you."

"Oh, Daddy, where have you been?"

"Who is that?" a loud voice called from the background.

"Daddy?" the girl said again.

"Baby, I want you to know…"

"Who is this?" A familiar voice shouted straight into my ear. How had I ever loved that voice? "Who is this?" she shouted again.

"Who do you think?"

"We have a legal agreement, Mister Miles," she shouted. "If you ever call here again…"

"Mother!" my daughter shouted in the background.

"Get her out of here!" the shrill voice commanded, and then switched back to the phone. "You son of a bitch, I thought you were dead for sure."

"She's my daughter!"

"Haven't you caused enough pain?"

"I've got some money now," I said.

"It's a little late for your money," she said, and the line went dead.

The neighborhood kids woke me on their way home from school. I lay there in bed listening to their laughter and fighting, and fragments of the night flickered through my mind. Relita. The cops. The sweetness of my daughter's voice followed by the nightmare voice of my ex: *I thought you were dead for sure.* And now she knew I wasn't. Was that good or bad?

I looked out the window. Irv, my dayman, had quit early. The cab was parked at the curb.

I showered and shaved, and went out to another grey day.

My first load was a nurse on her way to Weiss Hospital. $2.80 on the meter; she gave me three and told me to keep the change.

I went south, heading for the business down in the Loop. Two short hops and I was on Michigan Avenue where a woman with a tiny shopping bag waved.

"Thank you so much," she said climbing in. "Union Station, the Adams entrance, please."

I worked my way through the Loop, through early rush hour traffic. Thousands of trench coats were heading the same direction we were, to the commuter railroad stations just west of the river.

There was $4.40 on the meter when I pulled up with a swarm

of other cabs. The woman handed me five dollars. "Keep it," she said.

A young black guy hurried over and opened the passenger door. He was clean and healthy looking, wearing a navy pea coat and sporting a thin goatee.

The woman started out, then stopped. "Driver, I'm sorry. Could you let me have one quarter, please."

I handed her a quarter and she dropped it into the guy's waiting hand. "Thank you," he said, and he closed the door behind her and held the same hand out to me. "Help the poor?"

"Whose quarter you think that was?"

I started away but then the black guy slapped the side of the car. "Got one for you," he shouted.

"Do you go south?"

It was an older black woman. She was lugging an old suitcase, one that looked like an oversized doctor's bag.

I waved her towards the cab, and the guy grabbed her suitcase and started around for the trunk.

"Put it in here." I reached back and opened the door.

The woman slid into the back seat. The guy slid the suitcase in behind her. "Thank you so much," she said, and she handed him a dollar.

She gave me an address on South Aberdeen and I pulled away trying to calculate what the guy might make on a good day. If you could make a buck and a quarter every thirty seconds for an hour…

"Where you coming from?" I asked, once we were on the highway heading south.

"Mississippi," she said.

"Good trip?"

"A funeral."

"Oh. Sorry."

"Long time coming," she said.

The address was in the heart of Englewood. But most of the neighborhood—like so many other neighborhoods on the South and West Sides—was pretty much gone. Half the buildings had disappeared. There were drug dealers and gangbangers on the corners. But the old woman lived in the middle of the block, in a well-kept six-flat, with a sturdy looking gate out front.

Ten dollars on the meter. She gave me thirteen.

"Thanks very much," I said, and started to open my door. "Let me help with your bag."

"No. No. You stay right there." She got out, then reached back for the bag. "Don't pick anybody up out here," she whispered. "Lock your doors. Go straight back to the highway."

I locked the doors, waited until she was through the gate, then I followed the rest of her advice.

I got stuck in a traffic jam on the way back to the Loop, then wandered around for a while, trying to stay away from the worst of the traffic.

I made a short hop from LaSalle Street to Union Station. The black guy was nowhere around.

An older guy in a suit and tie flagged me on Wacker Drive. As we headed for Lincoln Park, he opened a newspaper. "They ought to give you guys shields," he said.

"This job isn't bad enough," I said. "Now you want us to drive around locked up in little cages all day."

"Whatever you say," he decided. $6.20 on the meter, I got $7.00.

On Lincoln Avenue, a familiar-looking guy was standing at a bus stop holding a small gym bag. As I stopped for the light, he stepped off the curb and looked up the street for a bus, then decided the hell with the CTA and pointed a finger my way. I waved him over.

"The Three-Six," he said, sliding in.

"You going to work?" I asked.

"Goin' to pick up the fucking cab," he said and he didn't sound very happy about it.

"Maybe I'll get something to eat," I said.

The Three-Six was a restaurant and cabdriver hangout just north of the Loop. There was a big parking lot that was often busier than the restaurant itself. If the dayman lived south and the nightman north, it was the perfect spot to drop the cab.

"You always do nights?" the guy asked.

"Yeah. How about you?"

"It's all fucked up, man. You know that?"

"Sure," I said. If you listened to some drivers everything was fucked up. They never made any money. If it was sunny they complained that people walked. If it rained they bitched that everybody stayed home.

"I just can't do these nights anymore," the guy said.

"I can't do the days." I knew how to bitch too. "I've tried but I can't deal with the traffic."

"You'd rather get shot in the fucking head?"

"I'm not sure," I joked.

"I got kids, man," the guy said. "Ain't nothin' funny 'bout this shit. You got kids?"

"Yeah."

"Then you know what I'm talking about."

"Sure," I lied. The truth was I didn't have a clue. I hadn't seen the afternoon edition of the morning paper yet.

The meter was pushing five dollars when I pulled into the parking lot of the Three-Six and found an empty space between two Yellows. "Just give me a couple," I said.

"Thanks, man," the guy said. He handed me three.

Inside, I nodded my head at a few familiar faces then slid

into a vacant booth. The waitress brought coffee. I ordered bacon and eggs.

"It's all about body language," a loud voice behind me said. "The assholes always give themselves away."

"But how?" a familiar voice asked. It was the rookie. He'd been on the streets for months but he was still a rookie.

"Usually it's something about the way they wave," the loud-mouth said. "Or the minute they open their mouth."

"But they're already in the cab," the rook whined.

"Don't pick up kids. That's the biggest thing. You see ghetto kids trying to flag a cab, you know something's wrong. You know they can't afford no ride. Let 'em take the CTA."

"I hope you didn't order the special," a new voice said. I looked up as Ken Willis slipped into my booth.

"Bacon and eggs," I said.

"Keep your fingers crossed, boy. Keep your fingers crossed."

Willis was a big, barrel-chested guy who still spoke with a West Virginia drawl after thirty years in Chicago. He'd driven a cab for several years back in the sixties, then switched to trucks. When the truck line had gone bankrupt during deregulation, Willis had come back to cabs while waiting for another decent trucking job to open up. Years had gone by and he was still waiting.

His hair was nearly gone and what was left was as grey as his face. A half smoked cigar sat unlit in a corner of his mouth. It might take him all night to finish it, and until he did he would keep it dangling there, spitting out flecks of tobacco now and then.

The waitress came by and filled Willis's coffee cup, then topped mine.

"Unbelievable, huh?" Willis said.

"What?"

"Polack Lenny," he said, as if that might mean something.

"What about him?"

"Oh, Jesus," he said, but then he didn't say anything. He looked off to the side, then towards the ceiling.

"What happened?" I asked.

"They found him by Cabrini," Willis said.

"Huh?" I still didn't understand.

"Shot in the head," he explained.

"Dead?" I whispered.

"What the hell you think we've been talking about?" the loudmouth wanted to know, and somebody passed a newspaper over.

"CABDRIVER SLAIN," the headline shouted. And there was a picture of Lenny's brand new cab, all the doors open so you couldn't read his name, and a bunch of cops standing around, probably laughing and telling stories.

"GOOD LUCK TURNS BAD," a smaller headline read. "The second cabdriver slain in Chicago this week was found shot to death early this morning on a dead-end street in the shadow of the Cabrini–Green housing project.

"Leonard Smigelkowski, who was recently awarded a taxi medallion in a lottery of fellow drivers, was found slumped over the wheel of his new cab by a security guard patrolling a nearby Commonwealth Edison substation.

"Smigelkowski, 56, is the fifth cabdriver slain in Chicago this year. Abdul Patel, 41, a driver for North Suburban Taxi in Skokie, was found stabbed to death early Tuesday morning in Garfield Park. His abandoned taxi was found several hours later in an alley a few blocks west of the park."

I remembered Lenny smiling and signing. *Look ma, no hands.*

"I just saw him," I said.

"When?"

"Last night."

"What time?" Willis asked.

"Midnight," I decided, "somewhere around there."

"They found him about two."

"He was deadheading up the Drive," I said. "He got on at Belmont and gave me the thumbs down. Said he was going home."

"You talked to him?"

I shook my head. "Hand signals," I explained.

"I wonder what happened?" Willis asked.

"Shit, he was going home."

"Yeah, but you know how it goes," Willis said. "Somebody flags you and you decide what the hell, one more load. You drop them off and somebody's waiting. Next thing you know you're back to work."

"Lenny was pretty careful," I said. "Christ, it doesn't make any sense. He never went into Cabrini." Lenny was one of those drivers who almost never picked up black passengers. He'd been fined and suspended several times.

"That's the scary part," Willis agreed.

The waitress dropped a plate in front of me. Two eggs stared back with sad, grease-covered eyes.

I pushed the food to the side and turned the newspaper to an inside page. There was a bad picture of Lenny, probably taken from his chauffeur's license, four for a buck and a half in the photo booth down at the Vehicle Commission. "Where the fuck is Hobbie Street?" I asked.

"Off of Crosby," Willis explained, "just south of that Edison substation."

"Jesus, what a place," I said. "Why the fuck would he go in there?"

"They stick a gun in your head, you'd be surprised the places you might go," Willis said.

I couldn't bring myself to eat the eggs. I made a sandwich of toast and bacon and washed it down with another cup of coffee.

We stood around in the parking lot, leaning against Willis's Flash Cab. "This fucking city," he said. "I don't know why I'm still here."

"Money," I said.

"You know, when I first got up here I really loved this town. I thought I had the world by the balls. Just drivin' around all day bullshitting away with whoever happened to be in the back seat. Christ, the money was easy back then: forty-two and a half percent of the meter and all you could steal. I don't ever remember working hard."

"Those were the days," I agreed, although I'd never worked as a commission driver. Back then, cabdrivers were regular employees. They got paychecks like normal people, had health insurance and other benefits. They even belonged to a union.

The union had been busted years before my time and the commission drivers were long gone. Today, everybody leased their cabs and paid for whatever gas they used. Anything over the lease and the gas was profit. There were no benefits, of course. The cab companies now considered drivers independent contractors.

"Yoo-hoo," a woman called from out on the street. "Taxi!"

"Where're you heading?" Willis called back.

"The train station," the woman said. She was young and white, wearing a trench coat and running shoes and lugging a thin briefcase. "Please, I've only got five minutes."

"You take her," I said. "I'm gonna head north."

But at Division Street, I changed my mind and turned west instead. I flipped my NOT FOR HIRE sign down, drove a few blocks and there was the city's most infamous patch, Cabrini-Green. There was block after block of nothing but dim government-issue highrises, surrounded by hard-packed dirt, and grey, litter-strewn parking lots which were usually empty except for a few junk cars. There were few trees, little grass, and hardly any people.

That was one of the most noticeable things about Cabrini. There were thousands of residents, packed into scores of buildings; but, with occasional—sometimes terrifying—exceptions, there never seemed to be many people around.

The top floors of the tallest highrises had been emptied out years ago, supposedly in preparation for remodeling. But the remodeling never happened and at night the place had the foreboding look of a ghost town. A spooky little ghost town, where snipers set up shop in deserted apartments and took potshots at whatever caught their fancy.

The victims were usually fellow residents. People who'd made the mistake of actually going outside; women and children, as often as not.

The place was a cabdriver's nightmare. It sat in the middle of some of the city's best cruising territory. The Gold Coast was a few blocks to the east, River North just south, and Old Town and Lincoln Park north. There was no way you could avoid the place. Several major streets skirted the edge of the project and three went right through it. Inside, there were narrow side streets and dead-end driveways where, over the years, several drivers had been found murdered.

When I was a kid, there'd actually been white people living here. But that was long ago. Now almost everybody was black, poor, and on welfare. The place was a boomtown, one day a month.

I caught the light at Larrabee and sat there, a full car length behind the car in front, giving myself plenty of room to maneuver.

This was the main intersection of Cabrini. On New Year's Eve the police would close both streets for blocks in every direction.

This did little to restrain the snipers on their biggest night of the year, but it did decrease the number of moving targets.

There were highrises on two corners, and a fire station on another. The most popular corner held a package liquor store. There was some local color lounging about and a few people waiting for the bus.

The light changed. I continued west and then turned south. This was Crosby Street, rutted with potholes and littered with debris. The substation was on my right behind a high cyclone fence. There were some small factories on my left, all closed for the night.

There were DANGER HIGH VOLTAGE signs sprinkled along the fence which turned in at Hobbie Street. I followed along. A large Bureau of Rodent Control sign joined the smaller signs. NO DUMPING, it warned. VIOLATORS WILL BE PROSECUTED. Across the way somebody had dumped a truckload of wallboard fragments and splintered lumber in a patch of weeds.

There was no sign of Lenny's cab or any clue as to where it had been found. The street ran west for about half a block but it didn't dead-end, as the newspaper had said; it curved and tapered into an alley that ran under the Ogden Avenue bridge and then out to Halsted Street.

I made a U-turn and started back the way I'd come. I didn't know what I was looking for. Some trace of Lenny, I guess, a guy I'd been having coffee with for years. A guy I'd laughed and joked with, just killing time, while waiting for dawn.

"Eddie, you take too many chances," he'd told me years before, after I'd described some close call on the South Side. But somehow he'd ended up here, on a street that was little more than an alley, within spitting distance of Cabrini. There was no way he would have come in here on his own. Not a chance in hell. Not Lenny.

I stopped when I got back out to Crosby. A block ahead, a twelve-story red brick building stared back. Even with lights burning in most of the apartments, the building looked dark and menacing.

A group of guys were hanging out alongside the building. They were all black, of course. Most of them wore hooded sports jackets, the gang fashion of the day. The hoods were up although it wasn't very cold. It was just part of the look, the fashion of intimidation.

They knew I was watching and soon they were all facing my way. The smallest of the bunch started to run towards me. He probably wasn't twelve. I took my foot off the brake and the cab started to roll. The kid stopped and strutted back to the group and there were high-fives and jive handshakes all around.

I turned right. Two blocks later I was surrounded by the world headquarters of Montgomery Ward. That was how quick the city could change. Two blocks and there was a white guy in a suit and tie looking for a cab.

I made a left and popped the door locks, and he slipped into the back seat. "LaSalle Street and take a left," he said pointing the way.

"You mind telling me where you're going?"

He gave me an address on LaSalle and I started that way. "Did you hear about that cabdriver?" he asked.

"Heard all about it," I said, and put an end to that conversation.

I made a left on LaSalle, dropped my passenger, and continued on as the street curved through Lincoln Park and out to northbound Lake Shore Drive.

I drifted into the left lane and pushed it up to about 70, thirty over the limit, passing everything in sight.

I took the Drive until it ended and then followed what should have been Lenny's route home, Hollywood into Ridge.

I'd taken this same route last night, a few minutes ahead of Lenny. But something or someone had turned him around.

I went under a railroad viaduct. The local 24-Hour Pantry franchise was in a strip mall on the left.

There were a couple of taxis parked on Ridge, but around the corner on Devon just about every car at the curb was a cab. Some belonged to private owners like Lenny. Others, to single-shift drivers who kept their leased cabs around the clock and worked whichever hours they preferred. Later, when the night drivers called it quits, there would be even more cabs.

This was a neighborhood full of taxi drivers, mostly Indian and Pakistani. But there were still some Jewish drivers, left over from the days when both the industry and the neighbor-hood had been predominately Jewish. There were a few blacks too, mostly Africans. And the occasional oddball like Polack Lenny.

There were three cabs parked at the curb on Lenny's street. I recognized two of them. One belonged to Ace, another to Tony Golden. Both were regulars at the roundtable.

I slowed in front of Lenny's two-flat. I'd dropped him off here a few times but I'd never been inside. The second floor was all lit up. There were people moving around beyond parted curtains. Somebody turned and looked out to the street. I con-tinued past and retraced my route to the 24-Hour Pantry. A sign over the door proclaimed: WE DOZE BUT NEVER CLOSE.

I filled a go-cup with coffee, carried it up to the counter, and slid a dollar towards a muscular black kid sporting a razor haircut and a plastic name tag which read Rollie. A skinny Indian or Pakistani stood a few feet behind him, arms folded, with a serious "I'm-the-supervisor" look planted on his face. His brass name tag read Mohammed.

"Hey, man." Rollie smiled and a gold tooth gleamed as he

rang up the sale. "I know you. You a taxi driver. You picked me up one time."

"Really?" I said. He didn't look familiar but that didn't mean anything. The passengers usually got a much better look at me than I got at them.

"You was cool, man." He handed me my change. "See, my uncle was sick and I couldn't get no cab to take me south. But then you came by. Yeah." Rollie smiled some more. "I tell you what. Next time you in, I buy the coffee."

"Anytime," I said, and I held up the cup. "Best coffee in town."

"See, wasn't for you, I might not of got to see my uncle that last time."

"You get a lot of cabdrivers in here?" I asked.

"Some nights."

"There was a guy might have been in last night," I said. "Older white guy, skinny, kind of reddish hair. You see anybody like that?"

He shook his head, "Most of our regulars be related to Mohammed here, you catch my drift." He smiled, and cocked his head towards the supervisor, who seemed not to hear.

I picked a newspaper off a stack, and opened it to the page with Lenny's picture. "How about this guy?" I asked.

"Oh, man, that the dude got killed?"

I nodded.

"Nah, man," he shook his head. "We was talking about that when I come on. See, everybody knew that guy they got a couple of months back. Used to be in every night. Little skinny, bitty foreign guy. Man, why would anybody kill a little man like that? You know he wouldn't put up no fight. You just blow him over."

I pointed to the picture again. "He would have been by just after midnight."

He shook his head again. "That's when I get off. Hey, Mo-hammed," he said, taking the paper from me and holding it up. "You see this dude in here last night?"

Mohammed barely looked then shook his head.

"You want I should ask the overnight crew?"

I shrugged, and dropped the paper back on the pile.

"He was your friend, huh?"

"Yeah." I picked up the coffee.

"Too many people out there got no heart, man," Rollie said. "No heart at all."

"You got that right."

"I thought about driving a cab one time," Rollie said. "But I got an uncle, different uncle, he used to drive a taxi and when I talked to him, he told me forget it."

"Smart man."

"Sometime," Rollie said. "But sometime he be dumb too."

"It's not much of a job," I said. "And once you get into it, it's hard to get out. Take my word."

"This here be the best job in the world." Rollie gave me a crooked grin and rolled his eyes towards Mohammed.

"I'll see you around." I started for the door.

"Hey, don't forget, man," Rollie said, "next time I buy the coffee."

"Sure," I said.

"Hey, what's you name?"

"Eddie," I said.

"I be Rollie," he pointed to his plastic tag.

DISCRIMINATION IN THE SOLICITATION, ACCEPTANCE OF, AND THE DISPATCHING OF SERVICE TO PASSENGERS ON THE BASIS OF RACE, GENDER, OR GEOGRAPHIC LOCATION OF PICK-UP OR DESTINATION WITHIN THE CITY OF CHICAGO IS STRICTLY PROHIBITED.

City of Chicago, Department of Consumer Services,
Public Vehicle Operations Division

I headed back south, to the streets I cruised night after night after night. From Wrigley Field down to the Loop, the Gold Coast to Lincoln Park, Old Town and River North—never straying too far from the lake—following Clark Street and Halsted, Lincoln and Wells. They were all nightlife streets and on good nights, they were loaded with white kids looking for cabs.

On Halsted, in Lincoln Park, a girl in an ankle-length coat waved. She had blond hair and wore her coat open, exposing a tiny skirt and long shapely legs.

"Cafe du Midi," she said sliding in. "You know where that's at?"

"I think I can find it."

"The last guy took me for a joyride."

I headed out Webster Avenue, a tree-lined residential street with a few bars and restaurants sprinkled around. I'd grown up right around the corner in a completely different world.

It had been a regular neighborhood back then, full of working stiffs like my father, a union printer. We were a little better off than most. My parents owned the building we lived in—a modest, red-brick three-flat—and we had the entire first floor. Upstairs each apartment had been divided in two.

When I was in high school, hillbillies and Puerto Ricans began moving into the neighborhood, and my father decided it was time to get out.

He sold the building and used the money to make a down payment on a vast six-flat overlooking Columbus Park on the far West Side in Austin.

My parents really loved that place, at least for a time. And my father was so proud of his business genius, replacing a dumpy, working-class three-flat with this palace where a doctor lived. "That's right," I once heard him whisper to an old friend. "A doctor!"

A few years later we could see the smoke from the riots in the black neighborhood a couple of miles east. The doctor was the first to go. In no time at all, the neighborhood was almost entirely black. My father held on, hoping to get his money out of the building, but he never did. My mother got her purse snatched one day and that was it. He sold the place for whatever he could get and they moved to the suburbs.

And my father never owned another apartment building.

And he never, ever, wanted to talk about Lincoln Park which had gone on to become one of Chicago's wealthiest neighborhoods.

The hippies had come around—about the same time the West Side was burning—with their little shops, coffee houses and clubs. Eventually they'd chased the Puerto Ricans and white trash away, and made the place safe for upper-middle class suburbanites who wanted to live near the Loop.

A few years back, somebody had gutted the dumpy old three-flat and converted it to a single-family home.

At one time more than twenty people had lived in that building. Now it was just one family. You had to be even richer than a doctor to pull off something like that.

A few blocks past the old homestead the street turned industrial. This was the one section of the neighborhood that still reminded me of the old days. On the edge of the river there was a string of leather tanneries loaded with Mexicans breathing chemical fumes, probably glad to be getting minimum wage.

We went over the river, under a railroad viaduct, and past more factories. We were the only car around.

"Where the hell are we?" the girl said, bringing me back to the present.

"This'll bring us right into Bucktown," I said.

"I feel like I'm in a movie sometimes."

"Where're you from?" I asked.

"Kansas City," she said.

"What brings you to town?"

"I just started a new job," the girl said. "Everybody's coming to Chicago. It's so cool."

"Where do all the jobs come from?" I asked. "I don't get that."

Factories seemed to close down every other week. Big plants with good, union jobs. Oscar Mayer. Stewart-Warner. Procter & Gamble. But these kids kept coming; suburban white kids for the most part, from Michigan and Kansas, Minnesota, Iowa and Ohio. And they kept finding jobs. Good jobs. White-collar jobs down in the towers of the Loop. Were they new jobs or were the natives being bounced? I hadn't been able to figure it out.

"There aren't any cabs in Kansas," the girl said as I turned left on Damen. "Here, you just raise your arm in the air and one stops. It's so cool."

Back at Clybourn Avenue, a movie was letting out and I was the only cab in sight. There were people on every corner yelling and waving their arms around. I stopped short of the intersection and watched the race.

The winner was a suburban-looking kid in a college sweatshirt. "Hold on," he said, sliding in. "I've got a friend out here somewhere." Then he shouted out the door. "Hey, come on. I got it."

A young guy in a sport coat slipped through the crowd. "I didn't know where you went." He sounded amazed.

"You've got to be fast in the big city," his friend said.

"Where to?" I asked.

"First I want to drop my colleague here at the Sheridan Plaza," the guy in the sweatshirt said. "Then I'm going to Fullerton and Clark."

"Be cheaper to do it the other way," I said.

"Let's do it my way," he said. "Take Clybourn, okay?"

"It's your money." I started down Clybourn Avenue, an old industrial street that had evolved into a shopping and entertainment strip.

We passed a row of tiny frame houses. There were some black people sitting on a porch under a large FOR SALE sign. A block down, a longtime black saloon had been transformed into a nightclub, full of white kids dressed in black leather.

Just past Ogden Avenue, the guy in the sweatshirt whispered, "This is it."

"What?" his friend wanted to know.

"Cabrini–Green," the guy whispered.

"Jesus," his friend said. Now he was whispering too.

We were skirting the northernmost point of the project. In front of a bleak-looking highrise, two black kids were jumping up and down on a pile of discarded mattresses. Nobody else was around.

The guy pointed to a boarded-up building on our left. "That's the only McDonald's to ever go bankrupt," he said.

"Why?" his friend asked.

"Because of all the crime," the guy said. Then he began to whisper again. "They killed a cabdriver in here last night."

"And you told him to go this way?"

"I come by here all the time," the guy said.

"Jesus, it's scary looking." His friend was impressed. "I wish I had my camera."

"I'll tell you one thing," the guy whispered, "you'd never catch me driving a cab."

"Boy, that's a relief," I put my two cents in.

"Were we talking to you?"

I slowed down a bit. "Why don't you get out right here, show me how tough you are."

"Why don't I write your number down and report you to the city?"

"Sure," I grunted. "Go ahead." It wouldn't be the first time.

They were right, of course. It was a scary looking place even on the brightest of days. What an ugly place to die, I thought, and I wondered again how Lenny had ended up down here.

For some reason, Rollie's words echoed in my mind. *Some people got no heart, man, no heart at all.* The kid had been right on the money.

In a window about fourteen floors up, a blue neon beer sign blazed away, the brightest light in all of Cabrini. I wondered if someone had an illegal bar up there for drinkers too petrified to leave the project.

If I saw the same sign in a Lake Shore Drive highrise I would assume it was some college student's room. But here,

I figured anyone smart enough to make it to college would also be smart enough not to make their window such an appealing target.

If they were really smart they'd get the hell out completely.

I turned left on Division, a street that led to the biggest bar strip in town, and we left Cabrini behind, just a dim reflection in the mirrors.

Sitting at the light at LaSalle, I found myself thinking about Rollie. The kid was all right, I decided. He could probably run a pretty fair hustle. He had the smile, that gleaming gold tooth, and the easy chatter. But instead, there he was playing it straight behind the counter of a convenience store.

And just like that, it hit me. I hardly knew Rollie, and here I was thinking of him like some long lost cousin. Christ, had he pulled some similar routine on Lenny? Was that what had happened? Was he the one who had conned the Polack down to the Green?

"Fuck," I said softly. I got sick of waiting for the light to change and made a right on red and headed south on LaSalle.

"Hey, where're you going?" the guy in the sweatshirt wanted to know.

"The Sheridan Plaza," I said.

"Why didn't you go straight to the Drive?"

I lifted my hand in a too-late-now shrug and turned left on Maple.

The meter read $5.70 when we pulled up in front of the Sheridan. "I'm getting out here too." The guy in the sweatshirt broke my heart. He handed me six dollars and waited for the change, then slammed the door.

I cruised north, thinking about Rollie.

Maybe I didn't remember picking him up because I'd never seen him before. It didn't take a genius to figure out I was a cabdriver. Not when I'd pulled up to the front door of the 24-Hour Pantry behind the wheel of a Sky Blue Taxi.

And if Rollie really did get off work at midnight, that's right when he'd need a cab. A few minutes to clean up, a few more minutes to bullshit with the overnight shift, and right about then Lenny would be walking through the door to pick up a newspaper, or maybe a six pack of beer. "Hey, Polack, remember me? I'm the guy who bought you that cup of coffee last week. You mind giving me a ride home?"

It would be hard to say no.

I exhaled, as if I'd been holding my breath all day, then relaxed in the seat. Maybe it was just a crazy theory but then again, maybe it wasn't.

Maybe the reason Rollie had decided not to drive a cab was because he'd figured a way to get the same money without the bother of actually getting behind the wheel.

At Division and Dearborn, a Yellow was angled towards the curb, picking up passengers. I was going around when the light changed. I stopped halfway into the crosswalk, a couple of inches over the center line.

An American–United Cab, making a left, was having a heck of a time trying to fit through the space I'd left. The driver, an old white guy with long, stringy hair, and the face of a heavy drinker, finally managed to line the cab up, then he crept forward slowly with both hands tight on the steering wheel. He had about a foot and a half to spare on either side.

As he pulled abreast, he looked my way. "Typical A-rab," he said, and he continued past.

All my relaxation went right out the window. "Hey, fuck you, you senile motherfucker," I shouted. "I could put a Mack truck through that hole."

His cab came to an abrupt stop and then started to back up.

I grabbed the mace. A limousine, following the cab, laid on the horn.

The cab stopped, the driver still a couple of feet beyond me. He stuck his head out the window. "Who you calling an old motherfucker?" he shouted. Brother, this was one ugly cab-driver.

"Who you calling an A-rab?" I asked.

"You drive like one," he said.

"And you drive like an old motherfucker, pal. You better find a new line of work."

I saw he was warming up to spit, but I had the green light by then so I stepped on the gas and got the hell out of there. "Dumb motherfucker," I said to myself.

I went up Dearborn until it ended at the foot of Lincoln Park, then switched over to Clark Street and continued north, the park on my right.

The cab business was not the business to get old in, I knew. I wondered how long the old guy had been driving. Thirty or forty years, I guessed, and now his reflexes were shot. His vision was almost gone and his judgment had taken the same one-way trip. He probably got robbed once a month and had passengers run out without paying every other night.

It was a glimpse of my own dim future, I decided. If I didn't figure something else out soon, or if someone—like my new friend Rollie—didn't shoot me first. Was that his game? I wondered. Was he setting me up with small talk and free coffee?

I kept driving but my heart wasn't in it. I couldn't keep my mind off Lenny, Lenny and my new friend Rollie.

I hardly saw my passengers. They were just people heading home from work, or out for the night. People complaining.

"Driver, shouldn't we have turned back there?"

"Driver, wasn't that a twenty I gave you?"

"Driver, where the hell you going?"

"I'm going to 1300 Grand Avenue, just like you told me."

"Granville," he shouted. "I said 'Granville.'"

"Oh, Jesus Christ," I said, and I flipped the meter off and made a U-turn.

The roundtable started early that night. When I pulled up, around twelve-thirty, there must have been twenty cabs parked in front of the pancake house.

The back table was full. Ace and Ken Willis moved over to make room. I slid a chair from a second table where the overflow sat.

"What's going on?" I asked. "There's still plenty of business out there."

"Some strange reason nobody wants to work," Fat Wally said. There was a pile of empty dishes in front of him and he was drinking straight from one of those metal milkshake canisters. It looked like a baby's bottle in his huge hand. We weren't dealing with any metabolism problem here. Wally liked to shovel it in.

"I still don't believe it," Ace said. He was a tiny old Jewish guy with a bald head and a neat, grey mustache. He'd known Lenny as long as anyone. "Christ, if they can get the Polack…"

And he left it dangling there.

"He fucked up," Willis said.

Ace shook his head. "Somebody conned him."

"But he fell for it," Willis said.

Ace lit a cigarette, the first one I'd seen him smoke in months. He was one of those guys who could never quite quit. "Kenny tells me you saw Lenny last night," he said.

"Right around midnight." I nodded, and I described the brief encounter out on Lake Shore Drive twenty-four hours before.

"Well, you're the last, so far," Ace said. "Jake saw him about eight, heading into O'Hare."

"Escrow." I winked.

Jake smiled back, and tipped an invisible cap. "Edwin Miles," he said. "The cabdriver's cabdriver."

"Morning, Eddie." Clair dropped a cup of coffee in front of me, then went around topping off the other cups. She'd just come on duty at midnight.

"Decaf." Tony Golden held up a hand.

"Oh, hell, you can't tell the difference," Willis said.

"Man, if I drink too much of this stuff," Golden held up the nearly empty cup. "I start throwing 'em out of the cab."

"Give him a double," somebody at the back table suggested.

"I was up along Ridge earlier," I said, "trying to figure out what might get Lenny to stop."

"Don't go looking for trouble, Eddie," Ace warned.

"There's that 24-Hour Pantry up there," I said. "I thought he might have stopped there on his way home."

"Not the Polack," Ace let me know. "He didn't like paying convenience store prices."

"Yeah, but say he just needed a loaf of bread or something," I went on. "This black kid works there. I asked him if he saw Lenny, you know, about 12:15, and he says no, he gets off at midnight. But what if he stood around talking for a while, and then Lenny comes in and the kid asks him for a ride home. I mean, if Lenny's in there all the time, he might do it."

"He wasn't in there all the time," Ace said.

"Here's the funny part," I kept going. "The kid comes up with some bullshit how he knows me. Says I picked him up one night when nobody else would. But I'll be damned if I remember him."

"Sounds just like you," Willis said, and he got the biggest laugh of the night. "You probably took him down to the Taylor Homes or something stupid like that."

The Robert Taylor Homes, on the South Side, were bigger and badder than Cabrini. And I'd been in there more times than I cared to remember. But some of the guys had never made the trip. Some of them went out of their way to avoid picking up black passengers. That included Tony Golden, the only black driver in the group. One of his favorite sayings was the punchline to Lenny's joke: "I don't go south."

Fat Wally would pick up anybody and go anywhere but he was a special case. His front seat was pushed as far back as it would go and it was so bent out of shape that when you got in his back seat you found Wally sitting right there with you. There wasn't enough room to sit behind him. He'd stretch his huge arm along the back of the seat and it would be inches from the passenger's face. Wally had been driving for almost ten years and he'd never been robbed. But people were always ducking out without paying. There, Wally didn't stand a chance. It took him about five minutes just to work his way out of the cab.

"How come it's got to be a black guy?" Tony Golden wanted to know.

"Not a lot of white guys robbing cabs," Alex the Greek said from the second table.

"Shit," Roy Davidson disagreed. "They're the only ones ever get me. The last son-of-a-bitch was wearing a suit and tie."

"It's kind of hard to believe it was a white guy got the Polack into Cabrini," Willis said.

"You've got a point there," Tony Golden said.

I tried to tell them about my trip into Cabrini to Hobbie Street but they never let me finish.

"Eddie, what the fuck's wrong with you?" Willis interrupted.

"It was early," I tried to explain.

Tony Golden shook his head. "You ain't never gonna learn."

"Tony, if you're so goddamn afraid, why don't you find another line of work?"

"Afraid? What do I have to be afraid of?" Tony shouted. "Nothing. 'Cause I stay right where I belong, and out of those shitbag neighborhoods."

"How many kids from Kansas can you stand?"

"What the fuck are you talking?" Willis wanted to know.

"Don't you get tired of tourists?"

"The trouble with you, Eddie," Ace started in, "you're still trying to work the old city. Forget it. The old city's gone."

"If it wasn't for tourists," Willis cut in, "we'd all be on welfare."

"The workable area of town is almost nothing," Ace went on. "It's a tiny little sliver. Figure it's from Irving Park down to the Loop, and from the lake maybe a mile inland. I'll bet the whole area ain't as big as Des Moines, Iowa. And that's how you've got to think of yourself. You're a Des Moines cabdriver, and if you get a trip out west or south and you can't get out of it, it's like being in Des Moines and going out to the countryside. When you drop your fare, you lock your doors and head straight back to Des Moines. No fucking around in between. Somebody tries to flag you, you drive right by. Sorry, buddy, I'm a Des Moines cab. You better call one of them West Side cabs out here."

"Amen," Tony Golden said.

"I've been telling you for years, Eddie, you take too many chances."

"Yeah," I said, "the Polack used to tell me that."

"Eddie, you may think you're smarter than the Polack," Ace suddenly sounded pissed off, "but I'll tell you something, whoever got Lenny could have gotten any one of us. The Polack was one very street-smart hack."

Nobody said anything for a long moment.

"Hell, I remember one time…" Fat Wally began.

But we never got to hear the story. "It's not so funny anymore, is it?" Paki Bob said.

"Don't start this up again," Willis said.

"It was all so funny when only foreign drivers got killed," Paki said.

"Come on, Bob," Ace said. "You know that's not true."

"My name is not Bob," Paki said.

"Yeah, well mine ain't Ace either but that's what everybody's been calling me for forty years."

"And I am not Pakistani," said Paki Bob, who was in truth a Berber from Algiers. When he'd first gotten in the business everybody had assumed he was Pakistani and someone had hung the nickname on him. By the time he'd had the nerve to correct them it was too late. This was the first time I'd heard him complain about the Bob part of his name.

"In my country," Paki said, "no one would ever kill someone for money. For politics maybe. For money, never."

Willis laughed. "In your country nobody's got any money."

"Oh, you lead such sheltered lives, you Americans."

"I like to be in America," Alex sang.

"How much you think Polack died for?" Ace asked.

"What's this about Lenny?" Clair asked as she pulled up with the pot of decaf.

"Don't you ever read the newspaper?" Willis asked.

"Dear Lord," she said softly, "that wasn't Lenny?"

She looked around the table. No one said a word.

"Oh, goddammit," she said, and she set the pot down way too hard and the glass shattered. The steaming coffee rushed out across the table. We all jumped to get out of the way, but Clair just stood there crying, the handle of the coffee pot, with a couple of jagged pieces of glass still attached, dangling there in her hand.

Violations of the following Rules and Regulations are Major Offenses: Solicitation; Refusal of Service; Deceptive Practice; Assault; Abusive Behavior; Operating Under the Influence; Reckless Driving; Failure to Surrender License; Bribery; Driving While License Suspended or Revoked; Failure to Display License; False Report of Lost License; Unlicensed Operation; Unlicensed Vehicle; Unsafe or Unclean Vehicle; Overcharging; Leased Vehicle Driven by Other Than Lessee; "Diving" - O'Hare; Unattended Cab - O'Hare.

City of Chicago, Department of Consumer Services,
Public Vehicle Operations Division

Even with Ace's words ringing in my ear, I couldn't stay out of the old city. He was right, I knew. Once you got away from the trendy lakefront neighborhoods, much of the city was garbage. But sometimes I felt more at home in the shabbier parts of town, cruising streets that reminded me of the city I'd known as a kid.

I was on Fullerton near California when an old white guy peeked out of a doorway, then raised an arm into the air. I pulled to the curb and he hobbled over, opened the door and leaned inside.

"A nickel to Logan Square?"

"It's gonna be a little bit more than a nickel." I waved him into the cab.

He was a little old man, shriveled with age. It took him a while to get in. First he backed up to the seat then he lowered himself slowly while holding the door for support. He lifted his legs, one at a time, and pulled them into the cab by hand.

Logan Square, where Kedzie and Logan Boulevards meet Milwaukee Avenue, was less than a mile away. The boulevards were tree-lined streets with broad parkways on either side. Large houses and stately two-flats were left over from another era.

This was one of the neighborhoods that real estate agents tried to promote as the next Lincoln Park. This was the great Chicago dream. Any crummy neighborhood might become the next Lincoln Park, where fortunes could be made buying buildings cheap from people like my father.

There was $2.20 on the meter when I stopped in front of a neat frame house, stuck between dilapidated apartment buildings. It didn't look anything like Lincoln Park. It looked like the next San Juan.

The old man dropped a five dollar bill over the front seat. "A nickel," he explained.

I killed the engine, grabbed the keys and the five, and walked around the cab to help him out. He went through the same routine with his legs, lifting them out one at a time. I held my hand out. He reached up, and I pulled him out of the cab.

He stood there breathing hard, holding the door for support. "Never get old, young man," he said after a while. "Never get old."

I reached into my pocket and pulled out two singles. "Here," I said. "You gave me too much."

He waved it away. "Keep it," he said. "Hell, I got plenty of money."

"Why don't you find somewhere else to live?"

"I've been here my whole life. Where would I go?"

A few doors down, a couple of punks were lounging in the doorway of a run-down apartment building. If the old man was lucky they would never hear about all his money.

I headed to Milwaukee Avenue and then turned southeast. Just past Logan Square, a guy in a fancy yellow jacket jogged across the street and stuck out an arm. I slowed to look him over. He had three strikes against him. He was skinny, which meant he might be a junkie. He was young, the age of most cab robbers. And he was Puerto Rican in a neighborhood loaded with Puerto Rican gangs. Everybody had guns.

But he was well dressed and he'd waved in a nice casual manner. I stopped a couple of car lengths past and he hurried up and opened the door.

"Thanks man," he said sliding in. "Thanks a lot."

"Where to?"

"California and Chicago."

"I'll drop you right on the corner," I said as I turned south on Sacramento. He looked okay but that didn't mean I wanted to take him down any dark side streets. And there were some very dark side streets just around the corner from California and Chicago.

"That's cool," he said.

"You making any money out here?" he asked a few minutes later.

It was one of those questions I hated to hear. "I just started," I said evenly, and I slid the canister of mace out of the ashtray and set it on my lap.

"Why you guys all so afraid?" he asked in a near whisper.

"Who's that?" I asked, and suddenly I could feel the blood pumping through my veins.

"Just seems funny that every time I get in a cab the driver just started."

"Maybe you're asking the wrong question," I told him.

"Okay, Mr. Cabdriver, what am I supposed to say?"

"Why don't you just sit back and enjoy the ride."

"Man, I've tried that. Just makes 'em more nervous."

"Well, when you get in a cab," I said, and then I stopped because I'd never really thought about it.

" 'Cause it's a real drag sitting back here and the driver's thinkin' I'm gonna rob him."

"You're not robbing anybody," I said as hard as I could.

"That's what I've been trying to tell you."

"I knew that before you got in," I went on with the show.

"How can you be so sure?" he whispered, and he leaned over the back of my seat.

I stretched my right arm out and dropped it on top of the guy's arms. He pulled them out from underneath and dropped back in the seat.

"I've been doing this for twenty-five years and nobody's robbed me yet." I was lying on both counts. "They've tried but they haven't pulled it off."

"Twenty-five years." He whistled. "You must be like Super Cab."

"That's me all right," I said, and he finally shut up.

A minute later there was some movement back there. I glanced in the mirror and the guy was completely turned around, looking out the rear window. There was nobody behind us and one lonely car two blocks in front. We were in the middle of Humboldt Park.

The last time I'd had a passenger look out the window like that, he'd turned back around with a knife in his hand.

I was doing about 45, fifteen over the limit. But where were the cops when you wanted them? I goosed the engine a bit and positioned the mace in my left hand, but it wasn't going to do much good if the guy had a knife or a gun. The trick was to keep rolling and not slow down. If we turned left at Division Street, I'd be heading out of the park.

The guy turned back around and then he just sat there. I couldn't figure out what he was waiting for.

Division was just two blocks ahead. This was the heart of the Puerto Rican neighborhood. It wasn't the safest part of town. But there was a 24-hour gas station at the corner of California. There would be cars and people. It would be the perfect place to throw him out of the cab.

A block before we got there I looked in the mirror and the guy seemed relaxed as hell. He was sitting back there watching me, with just the hint of a smile on his face. It was like he was waiting for me to throw him out. As if he could read my mind.

The light turned green in front of me, and just like that, I figured out the game. "How many free rides you get with all this bullshit?" I asked as I turned right. I looked in the rearview mirror and he broke into an easy grin.

"Oh, you know, sometimes it works," he said.

"You must get bored awful easy."

"Stop right here," he said.

I angled towards the curb, a half mile short of where he'd told me to go. "Three-twenty," I said, and I turned with my right arm up on the back of the seat, the mace ready in my left hand.

He handed me four singles.

"Keep the change, guy." He smiled, and then sat there with the door open, one foot on the pavement. "One guy shit his pants, man," he said. "I could smell it. You believe that, man? He shit his pants."

I didn't say anything. He got out and closed the door.

"Yo," he called.

I turned and he stuck out his hand like it was a gun, pulled the trigger and broke into laughter. I held up a middle finger, made a U-turn, and drove away.

I headed east towards the lakefront. It was the one part of

town where—day or night, rain or shine, good times or bad—
someone always wanted a cab.

I was on Diversey in Lincoln Park when a young couple,
clean-cut and white, stepped out of a 24-hour drugstore. The
guy was wearing extra-large shorts and a flowered shirt. He was
trying to pretend that he wasn't cold. The girl had been smart
enough to wear a jacket. She lifted the hem of her skirt several
inches and stuck out her thumb.

The guy held the door open and the girl climbed in. "Hey,"
she said in a low, raspy voice. She had blond hair and a nice
smile.

"Hudson and North," the guy said. "Go through the park."

"Be cheaper to go the streets," I said.

"Yeah, but I got my baby with me," he said in a low voice.
"The park's more romantic."

"Oh, baby," she whispered, and she fell into his arms.

I headed east, then followed the curving lanes south through
Lincoln Park. We passed the zoo. None of the animals made a
sound, but I heard the guy say, "A bed is a very personal thing."

I looked in the mirror. The girl smiled back. "That's why I
love him," she said. "He says the dumbest things."

"This girl doesn't have a bed," the guy let me know. "You
believe that? She spent every last dime to buy a house in the
worst neighborhood in town and now she doesn't have enough
left for a bed. We have to sleep on a couch."

"Why don't you tell him why we go to my place?" the girl
challenged him.

"Oh, I think he can figure that out," the guy said.

"I get the picture," I agreed.

"We go to my place because his apartment is such a mess we
can't go there," the girl explained. "I mean, he's got dishes that
haven't been washed in months. The place smells like the

inside of a laundry hamper. There's dirty clothes everywhere, and," she paused dramatically, "he's got roaches." She whispered the last word.

"Now why'd you tell him that?" The guy sounded honestly hurt.

"Oh, he doesn't care," the girl said.

"As long as you're not my neighbor," I said. "You guys getting out at the corner?" I asked as we got close.

"That's great," the girl said.

"Fuck that," the guy said. "Turn left at Sedgwick and come in off Blackhawk. I ain't walking around out here."

"It's not that bad," the girl said.

"It's all fucking black," the guy disagreed.

"Not for long," I said as we turned. The south side of North Avenue was still mostly black, a buffer zone between Cabrini-Green and the white world. North of North Avenue the neighborhood was mainly white and wealthy.

"See, that's what I've been telling you," the girl said. I made two rights and we drove up a block of small houses and two-flats. "They won't be here forever. Besides, most of them are very nice."

"Right here," the guy said.

"You're just a big bigot," the girl let him know.

"Four-seventy," I said as we stopped in front of a small brick house. The guy handed me six.

I worked the late bars until they closed and before long even the bartenders were home.

I was on State Parkway, just past the Cardinal's mansion, when a big, healthy-looking guy with a head full of thick, black hair and a puzzled look on his face staggered out from between parked cars.

He stumbled over to the driver's door, drunk as a skunk, and smelling about as bad. "Christ, this is so stupid," he said. "I'm looking for my car."

"Where'd you leave it?" I asked.

"Somewhere 'round here," he mumbled.

"You got any money left?" I asked.

He searched his pants first, then his sports coat. After a while he found some bills in an inside pocket. He said something I didn't understand and waved the money around.

"Well, why don't you give me some of that and we'll drive around and see if we can find it," I suggested.

He peeled off a twenty and held it out tentatively. I snatched it out of his hand and then reached back and opened the door. It took him a while to get in, and then a while longer to close the door, but finally he was all settled and I started driving.

State Parkway was a street of swanky highrises and old stately greystones. It was the kind of neighborhood where a parking space would probably rent for as much as my apartment.

"What kind of car we looking for?" I asked.

"Red," he said.

"Well, that narrows it down some," I decided. "You gonna know this thing when you see it?"

He didn't answer.

I glanced in the mirror. He was sitting crooked. His feet were still over by the left door but his head was all the way on the right side, flopped against the back of the seat. His eyes were open but they wouldn't be for long. "You can't sleep in here," I said.

"Huh?"

"Come on, sit up straight." I reached back and tried to straighten him up.

"What're you doing?" He shook me off and straightened up a little on his own.

"I'm trying to find your car but you won't tell me what it looks like."

"Red," he said again.

"You're a big help, pal." I lowered all the windows, hoping the cold night air would keep him awake, then drove slowly down the street.

We passed plenty of red cars, and the old Playboy mansion and the Ambassador Hotel, but the guy never said a word. At Division, I turned right and drove past the bars, all closed for the night.

"You wan' a nightcap?" the guy mumbled.

"They're closed, pal," I said. "They're all closed."

I made the right on Dearborn and cruised slowly up to the end of the street which put us just west of where we'd started. "Where do you live?" I asked.

"Cleveland," he said sadly, and I knew he didn't mean the avenue.

"Too bad," I said, and then something occurred to me. "Wait a minute," I said, "is this a rental car?"

"Hertz," he said.

"Oh, fuck them," I said. "Call 'em in the morning and tell 'em somebody stole it. Where you staying?"

"Hyatt," he said.

"Which one?"

He hiccupped. "O'Hare."

"That's perfect," I said, and I switched the meter off and back on and started out down North Avenue. There was hardly any traffic. Most of the drunks had made it home and the day people were still snug in their beds.

Just before the river, a tall, black hooker, in white short-

shorts and a shiny white vest, was leaning against the brick wall of a shuttered factory. As we approached she opened the vest wide, exposing two enormous breasts.

I tooted the horn.

"Sweet, Jesus," the guy moaned. "Get a load of those tits."

"She's got a set alright," I said as we headed over the river, past the old Procter & Gamble plant, now closed and FOR SALE.

"Wait a minute," the guy said. "Stop!"

"Huh?"

"Go back."

"You out of your mind?"

"I want some nigger pussy," he said with a bizarre southern accent.

I didn't slow down. I made the light at Elston, barely slowed for the light before the expressway, made a right on red and hit the ramp leading towards O'Hare.

"Where the fuck you going?" he shouted.

"I'm taking you to your hotel," I said.

"Asshole," he said. But then he relaxed. We were doing 65. What was he going to do, jump?

"Christ, did you see those tits?" he asked after a while. "I mean were those tits or what?"

"She had a set," I had to agree. "She definitely had a set."

Nobody said a word for a while. We cruised along, out there in cabdriver heaven, no traffic, no stop lights, not a word from the back seat. The meter was pumping like a heartbeat, twenty cents every few seconds. Little flashes of red adding up to a buck twenty a mile. Better than seventy-five dollars an hour at this speed. If I could just find a way to stay on the highway and keep the damn thing turning all night long.

"Three days," he said after a while. "You believe that?"

"Whatever you say," I said.

"I used to be out for weeks," he said. "I don't know how I did it."

"We're almost there," I said.

"Jesus, Mary and Joseph," the guy said softly.

"Sixteen-forty," I said, when we pulled up at the hotel. The twenty was to look for his car. The trip to the hotel was a separate matter.

He went searching through his pockets again and finally found the roll. He looked from the bills to me, to the meter, back to the bills.

"Sixteen-forty," I said again.

He still looked puzzled. "What happened to the car?"

"You decided to call Hertz in the morning," I said. "It's sixteen-forty."

He pulled another twenty off the roll and held it out. I grabbed it. "Sixteen-forty. Out of twenty," I said. But I didn't move to make change.

He looked at the bills again and dug through and found a five. I grabbed it before he could change his mind.

"Thanks," I said. I got out and opened his door. "Welcome to Rosemont."

It took him a while to get out, and all the while he was struggling I was watching the floor where a couple of bills were getting trampled under his feet.

"Three fuckin' days," he said as he staggered towards the lobby.

I waited until he was through the revolving door, then I reached into the cab and picked up the bills. Two singles. Well, it was hard to complain. I'd gotten forty-seven bucks for a twenty dollar trip.

I know there are people who would say I was a thief and they could probably make a case. But I didn't hit him over the head. And I didn't let him get behind the wheel of a car. And he didn't end up face down in an alley with all his money gone and a case of AIDS to boot.

I was a cabdriver. I did my job. I got him home.

I was on Lake Shore Drive and there was Lenny, out in the left lane, driving with no hands. Something moved and I spotted a black guy hiding in the darkness of his back seat.

"Lenny!" I tried to warn him. But he didn't seem to hear. He kept smiling and waving his arms around.

A balloon appeared in the back window and now I saw that it wasn't a guy at all. It was Relita. She was holding the balloon with one hand and playing a game of peek-a-boo with the other. She lowered her hand and flashed me a sparkling smile. I looked back at Lenny. He had a gun in his hand. He waved, pointed the gun at his own head and pulled the trigger.

The next afternoon, as I cruised through the busiest intersection in shabby Uptown, two black kids began to wave. They were about sixteen and everything about them was wrong. They were both skinny, dressed in dark, ill-fitting ghetto rags, and obviously dirt poor.

Lenny's murder had been all over the newspapers and TV and everybody was talking about all the cabdrivers getting robbed. And these two punks were so excited with their plan that they couldn't keep still. The guy on the far side of the street was jumping up and down so much that he kept scaring the neighborhood pigeons into brief, low-altitude flights.

When I waved them off, they didn't try to argue or show me their money. One turned to Broadway, the other to Sheridan Road and they started up again, waving away. It didn't make any difference which way the cabs were going. Hell, they weren't planning to pay.

But they were having a hard time finding a taker. Drivers were dropping their NOT FOR HIRE signs, turning their top-lights off and locking their doors. It was hard to imagine that anyone would ever stop. But I knew, if the kids could just tough it out, sooner or later someone would.

As likely as not, it would be a foreign driver. Somebody who came from a country where no one would ever kill just for money.

Lenny wouldn't have stopped for them in a million years, I knew, but he'd stopped for someone.

The kids weren't the only ones having trouble getting a cab. Just south of Irving Park, a husky black guy in jeans and a nylon windbreaker was hurrying south alongside the parked cars. He stuck out his arm but barely slowed down. One look was all I needed. This was a man who worked for a living. And he was going where he was going whether I took him there or not.

"I'm just going down to Belmont," he said. "Man, I didn't think anybody was ever gonna stop."

It was a familiar story. Every time a driver got killed certain people found it nearly impossible to get a cab.

"Two-twenty," I said when we got there.

He handed me a five. "That's yours," he said.

On Clark Street, a well-dressed black woman waved, then approached the cab. "Are you for hire?" she asked.

"Come on," I said, and reached back and opened the door.

"What is wrong with you cabdrivers?"

"Huh?"

"Six cabs just passed me by."

"Lady," I started.

"Do I look like a criminal?"

"Lady," I tried again.

"Now you answer my question. Do I look like a criminal?"

"Lady, if you looked like a criminal I wouldn't have picked you up. Now would you mind telling me where you're going?"

"I'm going to the I.C. Station," she said. "I live in the suburbs. I am not a criminal. I have never been a criminal. I do not associate with criminals. I have a good job. I pay my taxes. I go to church. But you cabdrivers, all you can see is the color of my skin."

"Lady, why you giving me a hard time?" I asked. "I'm the guy who stopped."

"Six cabs," she went on and on. "And I have each and every number and tomorrow morning I am reporting each and every cab to the Department of Consumer Services. What I don't understand, what I cannot fathom at all, is that two of the drivers were black themselves. Now would you please tell me why a driver would pass up someone of his own race?"

"Lady, black drivers get killed just as often as white drivers."

"But they can't seriously think I would harm them?"

"No," I agreed. "They probably figured you were going to some crummy neighborhood where they didn't want to be."

"And why did you stop?"

"I stop for just about everybody," I told her the truth.

"Well, thank you so very much," she said, and that put an end to that conversation.

Four-sixty on the meter. I got five.

The door never closed. A businesswoman slid into the back seat. "North and Sedgwick," she said.

I continued west on Randolph, through the Loop, then

turned north on Franklin. "Hey, didn't I have you last night?" the woman asked.

I glanced back but she didn't look familiar. "I don't think so," I said.

"Sure, I did," she said, and she leaned over the front seat to look at my chauffeur's license, which was in a plastic holder for all the whole world to see. "I remember your name. Edwin Miles. I remember thinking that was a really appropriate name for a cabdriver."

"Eddie," I said.

"You were telling us how Hudson Street was going to get better, remember? That's where I'm really going, Hudson south of North Avenue."

I turned around. "You're the girl without the bed."

"That's me." She smiled but she didn't look anything like the night before. She was wearing thick-rimmed glasses. Her blond hair was pulled tight and tied in back. She looked like a librarian in a very serious library.

"You're all dressed up," I said.

"A girl's got to make a living," she said.

"Yeah, but…"

"What?"

"Nothing."

"Come on." She smiled. "What were you going to say?"

The smile was hard to resist. "It's just that you're hiding all the good stuff."

"You really think so?"

"No doubt about it."

"How about now?" she asked a moment later. I turned around and her hair was undone and the glasses gone. Just like a bad movie, she was a knockout again.

"Now why would you want to hide that?"

"One of my rules," she said. "Never let the people at work know who you really are."

"Where's your friend?"

"Oh, him," she said. "He's probably sleeping, the bum. He keeps me up all night and then I've got to go to work and pretend to be awake. And he just lies around and sleeps the day away."

"Sounds nice," I said.

She leaned over the front seat. "You really think my neighborhood will get better?"

"Absolutely," I said.

We made a little jog at Division Street, keeping Cabrini to the west, and headed up Sedgwick, past Oscar Mayer's original plant, a huge red-brick place that had recently closed for good.

"This must be a neat job," she said.

"It has its moments."

"Me, I see the same boring people, day after day."

"Lots of boring people get in this cab," I let her know.

"Do you ever get lucky?"

"Huh?" I glanced over, and she had this teasing little smile on her face.

"You know, with women," she said.

"Not in the cab." I shook my head.

"That's funny," she said, and she dropped back in the seat. "I would think that women would…you know, I mean, you're pretty attractive…"

I glanced in the mirror and caught that same smile. "Thanks." I fell into the trap.

"…for a cabdriver," she added the punch line.

"Hey, thanks a lot, lady."

"Just kidding," she said. "Now tell me the truth, when was the last time a woman came on to you?"

"You thinking of inviting me in?"

"Can't," she said. "The bum's there."

"Just like to tease a guy to death?"

"You look like you can take it."

"I guess so," I said as I pulled up in front of her house. "Well, maybe I'll run into you some other time."

"Sure, just keep driving around," she said. "I'm always looking for a cab." She dropped some money over the front seat and flashed another smile.

Next door an older black couple was sitting on the porch of a tiny, ramshackle house. If they owned the place, they'd make a nice profit when they sold.

The girl walked up the steps and opened the door, then waved. I flashed my toplight and pulled away.

Public Chauffeurs shall be courteous to passengers, prospective passengers and other drivers at all times. Chauffeurs shall not assault, threaten, abuse, insult, provoke, interfere with, use profane language or offensive gestures around, impede or obstruct any person in connection with the operation of their vehicles.

City of Chicago, Department of Consumer Services,
Public Vehicle Operations Division

The funeral home was on Milwaukee Avenue, in the heart of the Polish section.

Lenny was laid out in a gleaming, silver-colored coffin that looked like it might do double duty as a one-man space capsule. The inside was all white silk, and there was Lenny in a dark blue suit, white shirt, and a blue tie sprinkled with tiny stars. His hands looked even bigger than in life. They lay one on top of the other, wrapped with grey rosary beads. His head was cocked to the side and I found myself wondering what the hidden side looked like.

I knelt down and made the sign of the cross. "Lenny," I couldn't help thinking, "how could you let them get you?"

He looked like he had never been alive. His face was covered with heavy makeup and was ghost white. His hair, which I'd always thought of as red, was now brownish-grey and it appeared to be glued to his scalp.

Above the casket there was a large photograph of an island in some lake, somewhere in the middle of nowhere. It was lit from behind, all trees and water and blue skies. You could almost see the angels fishing.

I made another sign of the cross, stood up, and headed for the door.

"Eddie." Ace caught me from behind. He was decked out in his funeral best, a suit a good ten years out of fashion.

"You look like an insurance salesman," I told him.

"And you look like a cabdriver," he said. I hadn't bothered with a suit. "Come on over and say hello to Nettie." He tried to turn me around. Nettie was the widow.

"Oh Jesus, Ace," I said. "I'm not any good at that kind of thing."

"Nobody is," he said. "All you've got to do is tell her how sorry you are."

"I'm gonna pass."

"Eddie, she wants to talk to you." Ace grabbed my arm and I could tell by his voice that he wasn't planning to let go. "You were the last person to see Lenny alive. Now come on over and tell her how happy he was, just like you told me."

"Fuck," I said, but I let him lead me a few feet. Then I jerked to a stop. Betty, my next door neighbor, was walking towards us. Now what the hell was she doing here? And where did she get that dress?

"Hi, Eddie," she said, and she leaned in and I gave her a little hug.

"Hey," I said, and then I ran out of words.

"I'm Betty," she said to Ace.

"Sorry," I said. "Ace, this is Betty. Betty, Ace. Betty's my next door neighbor."

"Call me Carl," Ace said. "Hey, didn't we meet a while back?"

"You remember, that's nice," Betty said. "Eddie brought me to the pancake house one night."

"That's right."

"I met Lenny the same night. I thought I should…"

"Sure," Ace said. "Come on, we're gonna pay our respects to the widow."

He took Betty by the hand and led her forward. I followed as they pushed through the crowd around a woman dressed all in black. "Nettie, this is Betty," Ace said, "and this is her friend Eddie Miles."

I'd been hearing her name for years and I think I had a picture in my mind of some old babushka lady. This wasn't her. The real Nettie couldn't have been more than thirty-five, which made her twenty years younger than Lenny. She was a tall, well-built blond—one of those healthy looking Poles—with clear blue eyes that shone right through her widow's veil. She spoke slowly, with a slight accent.

"Thank you for coming." She hugged Betty then extended a gloved hand towards me.

I took the hand and held it, and mumbled how sorry I was. She pulled me to her side.

"Oh, Eddie Miles," she said sadly. "Many times I have heard your name."

"He was a good guy," I said, and I started to mumble on but she stopped me.

"Now tell me when you talked, the last night."

"We didn't really talk," I started to explain.

"No. Carl has told me," she smiled. "That special way of cab-drivers."

So I tried my best to describe the night on Lake Shore Drive. I probably exaggerated a little. Lenny's smile, his playful mood. Her face glowed and a few tears rolled down her cheeks.

"I don't understand this no hands," she said, and she held out her hands and imitated me as I'd imitated Lenny taking his hands off the steering wheel.

I tried to explain how as kids riding bicycles we would take our hands off the handlebars and call to each other, "Look Ma, no hands."

"You wouldn't really say it to your mother," I said. "That was the joke, I guess. You'd never ride that way around her or she'd probably have a heart attack right on the spot."

"I understand," she said. But she looked confused. "And if he was coming home how did he...that place..."

"I don't know," I shrugged.

"My husband hated that place," she said. "He would tell me how he had to hurry past, and the people and the filth. When I hear that name now I begin to shake."

"It's a hellhole," I agreed.

"What does it mean?" she asked.

I shrugged. Who could answer a question like that?

"This Cabrini, what kind of name is that?"

"Mother Cabrini," I said. "She was a nun years and years ago." There was a small hospital out in the old Italian neighborhood, and a tiny side street, both named for the same woman.

"And why did they put this terrible place in her name?"

"She helped the poor, I think."

"And this was her reward?"

I shrugged again. What could I say?

"What a city, Eddie Miles." She began to weep. "What a horrible city."

"I'm so sorry," I said, and I stood there not knowing what to do. Betty hurried over and put her arm around Nettie. I tiptoed away.

Ace came up behind me. "Hey, I almost forgot, the cops want to see you." He dug through his wallet and pulled out a business card. I had one just like it. "Detective Hagarty," Ace said. "He's over at Belmont and Western. He said call or stop by after midnight."

The lobby was crowded with people talking and smoking. I heard Escrow Jake's voice, "When you're talking about cab-drivers, you got white guys, you got black guys and you got foreign guys." I looked over. The rookie was hanging on every word. "Now a black guy from Africa or Jamaica or somewhere, he's not black he's foreign. And a guy like Polack Lenny, he's been here so long, he's not foreign, he's white. Got it?"

The rook had a puzzled look on his face. He didn't get anything.

"They might have used the baby trick," someone else said.

"What's that?" another driver asked the question for me.

"You're driving along and a lady with a baby waves," the first guy said. "Nice guy that you are, you stop and she gets in and tells you where she's going. You go a block or two, not very far, and suddenly she gets very excited, 'Driver, stop the cab! Stop the cab!' You think there's something wrong with the baby, so you stop. She opens the door and gets out and leaves the baby on the back seat. 'Hey, Tyrone,' she calls to some guy who's been waiting for you to show up, 'you need a ride?' Well, you can't drive away with the baby in the cab. So the next thing you know you've got Tyrone sitting behind you. That's the baby trick."

I wandered on.

"I go whichever way the customer wants to go," an old grey-haired guy explained to another circle of drivers. "It's their money. I'm just trying to earn it. I always ask, 'Do you have a preferred route?' Man, I've had people take me on some of the most godfangled trips. Some of them have no idea at all how the streets work."

Alex the Greek stuck his head out of the circle, winked, then turned back to the old guy. "You're telling me that if someone wanted you to go up North Michigan Avenue the last Saturday before Christmas, when it's absolute gridlock, you'd do it?"

The old guy nodded his head. "I go whichever way the customer wants to." He sounded as if he'd said the same thing a thousand times. "It's their money. I'm just trying to earn it."

"Fuck that," I said, and I followed Alex out the front door.

"Guy doesn't have a clue," he said.

Ken Willis walked up, puffing on a cigar. "Come on, I'll buy." He pointed to an adjacent tavern where a sign read, *Zimne Piwo*.

"I can't," I said. "I've got a friend inside."

"Come on, Eddie," he said. "A Polish wake is the same as an Irish wake or a hillbilly wake. Why do you think there's a saloon next door?"

"I'm not much of a drinker," I said.

"What are you gonna do with all that money?"

"What money?" I asked, and they both laughed.

"Just have one," Alex said.

"What the hell," I said, and we all walked next door.

"To Lenny." Willis held up a shot of whiskey.

Alex and I raised our beers, "To Lenny."

"So who's the tomato?" Willis asked after he'd downed his shot.

"Oh, just my next door neighbor."

"Doin' the neighbor, huh?"

"Good work," Alex said.

"You guys ever hear about the baby trick?" I asked, and then explained it.

"Sometimes I think it's all part of some enormous plan," Alex said when I was done. "Remember a couple of weeks ago, that Friday night it snowed? About one in the morning I pick up this girl on Halsted. She's drunk. She's got no coat, no hat, no boots, and no money, and she wants me to take her way the fuck out to Irving and Austin."

"Fat chance," Willis said.

"That's what I told her," Alex said. "But she kept begging me. It's an emergency, she says, can't I please help. I don't know why but for some reason I really believed her, so I said okay."

"Chump," Willis said.

"What happened," I explained, "is she spent all her money on booze and now she wants a free ride home."

"Exactly," Willis agreed.

"All the way out I'm kicking myself," Alex went on with the story. "I mean, there's business all over the lakefront and here I am heading out to the fucking Northwest Side in the middle of a blizzard and I'm not even getting paid.

"On the way, I turn the radio on, and believe it or not, they're calling an order out that way so I take it.

"I drop her off and go to the radio call. It's only a couple of blocks away. I beep the horn. This guy comes out. They decided they don't need the cab, he tells me. But he hands me twenty bucks. 'Thanks for coming out in the snow.' Shit, he just paid her fare, round trip. I'm telling you, sometimes I think it's all one big test and you either pass or you fail."

"Lenny must have failed," I said.

"No. No. I don't mean like that," Alex said.

"Big time," Willis agreed.

No passenger shall be permitted to ride on the front seat of the taxicab unless all other seats are occupied or unless written authorization from the Commissioner is in the possession of the passenger. At no time shall more than one passenger ride in the front seat.

City of Chicago, Department of Consumer Services,
Public Vehicle Operations Division

Front seat riding was one of the Vehicle man's favorite tickets. So Betty was sitting in back, smoking and very clearly not saying a word, as we cruised east down Montrose Avenue.

"What's wrong?" I asked after a while.

"Your neighbor?" she said. "I can't believe you introduced me as your neighbor."

"But we are."

"Aren't we friends, Eddie?"

"Well, sure."

"Well couldn't you say, this is my friend Betty. I mean isn't that a little more than just your neighbor?"

"I guess so," I admitted. "Sorry."

"I know we're not exactly boyfriend and girlfriend but I hope I'm more than just the neighbor you fuck on Sunday mornings."

"Come on. I never said anything like that."

"Because if that's all I am…"

"Betty, we're friends," I said. "You know that. And you know I think you're great."

"I think you're great too," she said softly, and she put her arm over the back of the seat. "Can I hold your hand while you drive, Eddie? Or is that against the rules too?"

I reached up and found her hand.

"You always look so different from back here," she said.

I caught her eye in the mirror. "Better or worse?"

"Just different."

We went past Horner Park and over the river, then stopped for the light at Western Avenue.

"You know, I heard his name so much," Betty said. "The Polack this, the Polack that. Him and Ace, you're always talking about. Who's the other one?"

"Who?"

"Your other friend, you're always talking about."

"Ken Willis?"

"How come he doesn't get a nickname?"

"Kenny."

"How come you don't have one?"

"They used to call me Fast Eddie, years ago. I guess I slowed down."

"Fast Eddie. That's nice. Would you like to come up and keep me company for a while, Fast Eddie? Or is that another one of those rules?"

"You know what they say about rules?"

While his Public Passenger Vehicle is in service, no Public Chauffeur shall leave his vehicle to join any assembly or crowd of people upon any public way, and when standing or awaiting passengers he shall at all times remain in the immediate proximity of the vehicle of which he is in charge, but not further than ten (10) feet away. A Public Chauffeur shall not park or leave his vehicle in any place to engage in dice, cards, or any other game of chance in or about the vehicle.

City of Chicago, Department of Consumer Services,
Public Vehicle Operations Division

The police station at Belmont and Western was a low brick building on the edge of a modest shopping center just east of the river. The street in front was posted NO PARKING and a large NO PUBLIC PARKING sign guarded a side lot. It was a few minutes after midnight when I drove past the signs and slipped into an open space.

Inside, two uniformed cops, both white, overweight, and balding, sat behind a large, square counter, jawing away. All they needed were some hot dogs turning on a rotisserie, a few stools, maybe some french fries and fountain drinks, and they could probably take in enough to pay their own way.

A sign read: DETECTIVE DIVISION 2ND FLOOR. I headed for the stairway.

"Help you?" a voice asked. I turned back towards the counter. A third cop, this one young and black, peeked out from behind a computer monitor.

"Violent Crimes," I said.

He waved me back his way and picked up a telephone. "Who're you looking for?"

"Detective Hagarty."

He spoke into the phone. "Hagarty there?" Then he twiddled his thumbs, holding the phone with his shoulder. "Somebody for you downstairs," he said after a while. He looked up. "Does he know you?"

"Tell him it's Ed Miles," I said. "The cabdriver from the other night."

He repeated that into the phone, then hung up. "Wait over there." He gestured towards a corner where a bench and an ashtray sat under a pay phone.

"Hey," I asked, "when this was Riverview, what was here?"

"Riverview?" He looked confused.

"Laughhhhhh your troubles away." One of the older cops mimicked a commercial that had run every summer for years.

"This was Riverview?" The black cop seemed amazed.

"Shit, I thought everybody knew that," the older cop said.

It had been Chicago's biggest and best amusement park. It had closed as usual at the end of the '67 season but never reopened.

The black cop took his glasses off and laid his head back, his eyes towards the ceiling. "We used to come when I was a little kid," he said.

"Yeah." The older cop smiled. "That's why they closed."

"That's right, isn't it?" The black cop came back to earth. "Scared all the white folk away."

"You remember what was here?" I asked the older cop.

He shook his head. "Must've been the freak show."

"How'd I miss that?" I asked.

"This is such a jive town," the black cop said.

"Used to be some city," the older cop said slowly.

"Shit," the black cop said. He stretched the word out, then slipped his glasses on and went back to his computer.

The third cop looked over at me. "See what you started?"

Hagarty walked up smiling. "Eddie Miles," he sang. "Born to be a cabdriver. What's up?"

"You wanted to see me," I said.

"I did?" Now he looked confused. "About what?" he asked suspiciously.

"Lenny Smigelkowski, I guess."

"You involved with that?"

"I saw him on Lake Shore Drive the other night."

"That was you?"

I nodded.

"Well, come on up," he said, smiling again. "You can tell us all about it."

I followed him back the way he had come. Behind us the older cop said, "You can be damn sure it wasn't no Tunnel of Love."

Upstairs there was a large, open squad room with about twenty desks, most of them unoccupied. Hagarty led me towards the back where two desks were covered with papers and files. Foster was typing away at a computer keyboard. White letters moved across a blue screen.

Hagarty gestured towards a chair. "Turns out Eddie here is the guy who saw Smigelkowski on the Drive," he said as I sat down.

"Christ, he's everywhere," Foster said, and he looked my way. "I was hoping you were here to confess to that Relita Brown number."

I shook my head. "Relita Brown," I said. "How is she?"

"Intensive Care," Hagarty said. "St. Lucy's."

"She's gonna be okay?"

"Eddie, Eddie," Hagarty said, as if I'd just stepped off the first spaceship from Mars. "This is your typical Chicago success story. She just turned seventeen but she's already been hustling for three years. Her mamma was a whore. Don't know nothin' about her daddy, probably just some trick. After her mamma OD'd she went to live with her grandmother, till she died too. So she moved in with an aunt who's also a whore. She grew up right there by North Avenue and got to watch all the girls in action. She's a nice kid for a hooker but that's what she is. Is she gonna be okay? Come on. She was never okay. Not one day in her whole fucked-up life."

"She's a prostitute?"

"North Avenue stroll," Hagarty said.

"Gonna have to find a new line of work," Foster said. "Hard to be a hooker without tits."

"I wouldn't bet on it," Hagarty said.

I was suddenly dizzy. I leaned forward and dropped my head into my hands. "He cut off her tits?" I said.

"Just one," Foster said.

"Oh, man," I said. Suddenly I knew what I'd been looking at the other night. Suddenly I could see. I tried to push the vision out of my mind.

"She was asking about you," Hagarty said as I looked up. "She thought you were an angel leading her up to the Pearly Gates."

"Hooker heaven," Foster said.

"She thought she was dead," Hagarty explained, "and then she saw the words 'Sky Blue' all lit up in the sky."

"My toplight," I said.

"This is not a girl who takes a lot of cabs," Hagarty said. "Hell, she can barely read. I think she was kind of disappointed when we told her you were just a cabdriver."

"Did you find the guy in the van?" I asked.

"You practicing for Sergeant?" Foster wanted to know.

"Just wondering," I said.

Hagarty shook his head. "Tit Remover Number Two is still on the loose."

"Number two?"

"Oh, sure," Hagarty said. "We had another one, what was it, ten, twelve, years ago?" He glanced at Foster.

"Before my time."

"Somewhere back then," Hagarty decided. "Had a little trophy case down in the basement rec room. There wasn't a white tit in the bunch. Something about these clowns and black titties.

"This guy's got his little rituals," Hagarty went on. "He likes to lay flowers on them when he's done. Probably what he was getting ready to do when you showed up. We figure he thought she was dead. If you hadn't shown up when you did, might be one less hooker running around."

"He's done this before?"

"Looks that way," Hagarty said. "We keep getting reports. Christ, he's been everywhere. Milwaukee, Gary, South Bend, North Chicago, even the Quad Cities. He was on the six-week plan, but these serial guys are funny. The more they get, the more they want, and then finally..." He held up an invisible branch, snapped it in two, and dropped the ends into a nearby wastebasket.

"About Smigelkowski," Foster said.

For what seemed like the hundredth time, I described our brief meeting out on Lake Shore Drive. By now I was embellishing the story quite a bit: Lenny seemed ecstatic. The hand signals went back and forth for miles.

Foster interrupted. "I think I've finally figured out why all these cabs are always weaving all over the road."

"My exact thought," Hagarty deadpanned.

When I finished Hagarty asked the obvious question. "So why didn't he go home?"

"I don't know."

"You're sure he didn't have a passenger?"

I remembered my dream. "Well, there could have been somebody hiding back there but…"

"No, that wouldn't make any sense," Hagarty decided. "He's heading north, and then he ends up all the way down by Cabrini. You know what's funny, you're the only cabdriver saw him after ten o'clock."

"What's funny about that?"

"It's not like it's Yellow Cab 6-3-4-5-7-8-9. His goddamn name is on the door. Somebody had to see him but we haven't gotten one fucking call. You guys are the worst. Don't you want us to catch this guy?"

"Look, you're a cabdriver," Foster said. "How could somebody get in your cab after you'd decided to call it quits?"

"Well, if you're heading home and somebody flags you, sometimes you'll ask 'em where they're going, and if it's on the way you'd probably take 'em."

"Okay," Foster said. "How about another?"

"Well, sometimes you're gassing up and somebody'll need a cab. Or maybe you stop to pick up a loaf of bread or something, and somebody in the store or maybe the guy behind the counter…"

"Got anybody special in mind?"

So I told them my theory about Rollie at the 24-Hour Pantry. Foster scribbled some notes. Hagarty had me describe Rollie as best I could. They both liked the gold tooth.

"Was there anything in the cab that might have come from a convenience store?" Hagarty asked.

Foster picked up a file and began to go through it. An eight-by-ten photograph now lay exposed on the desk.

Lenny was stretched out like a V, his legs and his head at different corners of the floor. He was lying on his side, his ass still on the front seat. His pockets were pulled out and papers were scattered around. There was blood everywhere. One side of his face was almost gone. But the eye had survived and stared back at the camera. The meter was frozen at $16.20, and I could hear Ace asking how much Lenny had died for.

Hagarty followed my eyes. "Shit," he said, and he reached over and turned the picture face down. "No reason for everybody to get sick."

"A roll of peppermint lifesavers," Foster said, reading from a sheet of paper.

"Half a roll, wasn't it?" Hagarty asked.

Foster consulted the paper. "Check," he said.

"It was just a thought," I shrugged.

"We'll check it out," Hagarty said. "You never know. Smigel-kowski might have had a whole bag of groceries and whoever shot him grabbed it along with the money. We're pretty sure whoever did him got in his cab somewhere around that store."

"Why's that?" I asked.

Hagarty looked over at Foster. Foster shrugged.

"An Indian named Raj got it about three months ago. We're pretty sure the same guy did them both."

"Why?" I asked, and I wondered if Raj was the guy that Rollie had known. The guy so skinny you could blow him over like a leaf.

"Well, for one thing, Raj was last seen gassing up at Devon and Ridge. Your buddy was last seen heading up the same way. They were both going home. Raj only had three blocks to go from the station to where he parked the cab. Who knows? He might have stopped by the 24-Hour. The only thing wrong is, Raj didn't gas up until after two, so if this Rollie gets off at midnight he would have been long gone by then."

"Was Raj the guy they found on the South Side?" I asked.

"No, that's one of the other connections," Hagarty said. "They were found within a half-mile of each other. Raj was over in Old Town on Goethe Street." He pronounced the street *go-thee*.

Foster corrected him, pronouncing it *ger-ta*.

"The guy behind the Oscar Mayer plant," I remembered.

"That's the one," Hagarty said. "What do you say?"

"Huh?"

"Ger-ta or Go-thee?" he asked.

"Whatever the passenger says," I let them in on my system, "I say it the other way."

"You must be hell on wheels," Hagarty said.

"It passes the time," I said.

"You still lugging that mace around?" Foster asked.

I nodded.

"You think it's gonna do any good?"

"I'm not planning to use it against a gun, if that's what you're worried about."

"What all the bad guys are packing," he said.

"Maybe I should get one," I said. This wasn't the first time that thought had crossed my mind.

"I wouldn't advise against it," Foster said.

"You ever hear about the cabdriver took out a fifth of the Most Wanted list?" Hagarty asked.

I shook my head.

"Must of been six, eight years ago." He glanced at Foster.

"Something like that," Foster agreed.

"They'd been doing 7-Elevens and liquor stores. Two jokers

just out of Pontiac, cellmates. Killed two clerks. Anyway, we were staked out all over town waitin' for 'em so they decided to switch to cabs, but they sure picked the wrong driver. Clayton something…"

"Thomas."

"Yeah, that's it. Clayton Thomas, nice old black guy. They pistol whipped him a bit, just for fun, and told him to drive way the fuck out to Harvey. Well, Clayton wasn't any fool. He knew they were never gonna let him make the return trip, and the thing was, he had a gun tucked away under a cigar box on the front seat. He managed to slip it out and then at a red light he turned around and just smoked 'em. They never got off a shot.

"We'd been looking for the guys for a week and Clayton solved all our problems in about half a second. And then he delivers 'em. He drives right to the station with the stiffs in the cab. We wanted to give him a medal. This was one tough hack. But a couple of months later he calls us. The city won't renew his license. Wouldn't tell him why. We went downtown to see if we could help out. They told us no dice. What was it that guy said?"

"We let cabdrivers carry guns," Foster mimicked some Consumer Services bureaucrat, "next thing you know, they'll be shooting little old ladies in fare disputes."

"See, Clayton's mistake was he told the truth about the gun," Hagarty said. "What you need is something that isn't registered. Then if you ever use it, just say you took it off the other guy. Nobody's gonna really care."

"Or find yourself a nice dark alley," Foster advised.

"Now don't give him any ideas," Hagarty said. "We've got enough work already."

Any driver who refuses a fare on grounds of NOT KNOWING where passenger's destination is, in addition to being charged with refusal of service under S28-28 MCC and this rule, shall be retested. Failure to pass the written test shall result in recommendation for revocation.

City of Chicago, Department of Consumer Services,
Public Vehicle Operations Division

It was one in the morning when I headed east towards the lakefront. Relita was a whore. Didn't that just figure?

I laughed at my own disappointment. What had I expected to find in an alley in the middle of the night, a choir girl?

On Sheffield Avenue, a cab light was flashing. People were milling about under a nightclub canopy. The ladies were in long dresses; the men in suits and ties. One cab was loading up and three empty cabs waited, blocking half the street.

I was going around the whole mess when an older guy stepped out from the crowd and pointed straight at me. I stopped and waved him over. The waiting cabs started honking their horns, the drivers yelling out the windows, but the guy didn't pay any attention. He shook a few hands, hugged a woman and walked right past the cabs and opened my door.

"Madison Street," he said, sliding in.

"Long street," I said as I started away. "Where to?"

"I'm not exactly sure," he said. "But I'll let you know when we get there."

"Gotta know where I'm going, pal." Rule number one.

He was a rugged looking guy, fifty or sixty, with thinning

grey hair and a slender white scar that ran straight down from one baggy eye. He caught my eye in the mirror, then a ten dollar bill came sailing over the back of my seat. "Humor me a little, okay?"

"Sure," I said, and I tucked the ten away. "But it really is a long street. Can you at least give me a hint?"

"Why don't we start at the beginning," he said.

The guy didn't say a word all the way down Lake Shore to Randolph Street. I turned left on Michigan, then made the next right. "Madison Street," I said.

"It's nice to get a white guy for a change," he said as we went under the elevated tracks.

We went through the Loop and across the river and then the highway. "Where'd they all go?" he asked a couple of blocks later. There were blocks of nothing but empty lots. Then several blocks where a few buildings had survived. Then more empty lots. "Christ, this used to be wall-to-wall winos," he said. "In the summer they'd be sittin' all up and down the sidewalk. I mean, there wouldn't be one empty spot. They'd be passing bottles of cheap wine back and forth. The smell was really something."

"Those were the days," I said. And I remembered that sickening smell, being trapped on a Madison bus on a hot summer afternoon trying not to breathe.

But the flop houses and the bars, the missions and soup kitchens, pawnshops and liquor stores, the little hole-in-the-wall joints, and the winos who had patronized them all, had been gone for years. One lonely day-labor house was the only hint that—not too many years ago—the largest Skid Row in the country had been right here.

"Probably all dead," he said.

"More than likely," I agreed. Dead and buried in Potter's Field, one on top of another in a long trench, cheap pine boxes, no marker, no mourners, the We Haul Anything Cartage Company instead of a hearse. Where have all the winos gone?

The surviving buildings were mostly dark brick and covered with old, rusted burglar gates. There were a couple of restaurant supply houses that looked like they'd been there before Skid Row. They'd waited out the bad times and now the rebirth of the Near West Side was approaching.

There was one new building right on Madison and a couple of remodeled storefronts. But for the most part the signs of the future were hidden away on the side streets, where several brand new office buildings stood. They were almost all one- or two-story jobs; secure-looking brick places, surrounded by large, fenced-in parking lots, illuminated by floodlights and monitored by closed-circuit TV's.

There were some people wandering around near Ogden Avenue. There was a drugstore, a liquor store, a Chicago Housing Authority senior citizen highrise, and a Kentucky Fried Chicken.

St. Lucy's Hospital was a few blocks south, just over the expressway. Relita was down there in Intensive Care. A typical Chicago success story. A trick baby who'd grown up too fast and followed in her mamma's footsteps.

Soon we were back to the empty lots. Some of these were actually paved or covered with gravel, parking lots for the Chicago Stadium. There was block after block after block of nothing but parking lots.

"The hockey team still play here?" the guy asked.

"Yeah," I said. "Basketball too."

It was a big grey-stone place that had been there forever. It had been the site of political conventions and prizefights, circuses and ice shows. It was about the only reason I ever ended up out this way. There were housing projects to the north and south; beyond it lay what was left of the West Side.

I hit the power door locks. "How much farther?"

"I'm not really sure," he said.

"The further we go, the worse it's gonna get."

"What are you so afraid of?"

"Somebody might want to take target practice."

"Who?" He laughed.

I had to admit he had a point. There was hardly anybody on the street. The buildings had been burned, bombed or otherwise destroyed and whoever had lived in them had, for the most part, disappeared.

The brick pickers had picked the whole bricks from the rubble and stacked them on pallets, and they'd been trucked away. Only the rubble remained on the West Side. Rubble and weeds, and junk dumped directly under NO DUMPING signs which were nailed to thriving stink trees.

The prairie was returning to Madison Street.

There was a burned-out record store, barely standing, near a fire station that hadn't been close enough. A storefront church was boarded up, and beyond that, we finally found a little action.

There was a line of cars. A nice orderly, integrated line, everybody waiting patiently for a group of black kids to lead them around the corner, one car at a time, to buy whatever drug it was that they just couldn't live without.

One of the kids whistled and waved as we passed, pointing us back towards the end of the line.

"Just like TV," my passenger said.

I skirted a crumbling stretch of pavement and my headlights exposed a lone streetcar track, set in sturdy red paving bricks, shining back from some long-gone city.

A couple of skanky hookers were lounging in front of a low viaduct. Was this what he was looking for?

One waved halfheartedly, as if she knew no one would ever again be interested. They both looked diseased and old, women that North Avenue or some other strip had already used up and thrown away. Was this Relita's future? Was this where you came when you only had one tit left to sell?

"Safer to go swimming in a sewer," my passenger said.

A squad car passed going in the opposite direction. Neither cop glanced our way and I wondered if they would pay any attention to the line of cars a few blocks ahead.

I glanced in the mirror. The squad turned south. We swerve and don't observe.

There was a father leading two kids Indian file down a crumbling stretch of sidewalk. The kids were about six and eight. They were having a great time dodging the holes.

There were a few cars at the curb but almost all were burned out or abandoned. Anybody who put enough money together to buy a car probably drove it straight out of the neighborhood.

There was a liquor store and then a storefront medical center, both with every window bricked up solid.

I didn't see a grocery store anywhere around.

"What is it you're looking for?" I finally asked.

"Damned if I know," he said. "Last time I was here was 1964."

"You're shitting me."

"Lived here most of two years," he said. " '63 and '64. People start talking about where they were when John Kennedy got shot, I tell 'em I was sitting in a barber shop on the West Side of Chicago getting my hair cut by a little I-talian guy name of Pasquali. Christ, I'll never forget. It took about two hours. He had a little black and white TV in the back room and we kept running back there every time something new came on."

"You're not gonna find any I-talians out here tonight," I said.

"No, no," he said. "I figured as much. Hell, years ago, I was changing planes at O'Hare. Had a couple of hours to kill, so I got in a cab and asked the driver to take me out this way. He flat out refused to go. Wouldn't leave the cab line."

"Can't say I blame him," I said.

"No," he said. "I gotta admit it's worse than I thought. But boy, you should have seen it back then. It was really something."

"Yeah," I said. "I know."

We were in the center of the riot zone now. There was nothing but rubble for blocks. But I could still detect the faint scent of charred wood decades after the last ember had died. I knew the smell was just a trick of memory but all the same there I was standing on the roof of the building my father loved so much. We were watching the smoke from the riot drift over our heads.

"The late, great West Side," I whispered to the ruins.

I wondered if my father had known what was coming, that day on the roof, as his great business sense went up in smoke. It had never, ever, been spoken of, and never would be now.

My old man, I thought, and I shook my head at all the things that had never been said.

A few blocks later, my passenger finally had enough. "You might as well turn around. It's not going to get any better. Why don't you take me to the Marriott."

"Downtown?"

"The one on Michigan Avenue."

I drove another half block and then started to make a U-turn in the middle of a deserted intersection. Up ahead, some red neon glowed from the only building on the block.

"Wait a minute," the guy said. "Let's see what that light is."

"Son of a bitch," he said as we got closer. MITCHELL'S was written in red neon script. An unlit Budweiser sign hung over the door. "Stop," he said, and I stopped across from the bar. "I can't believe it's still here."

"You can bet there's a slightly different crowd."

"Same name."

"Too cheap to buy a new sign," I said.

"Let's go in and have a few," he said.

"Yeah, right." I laughed.

He threw a twenty over the seat. "Stick that in your pocket and I'll buy the drinks."

"Tell me you're kidding," I said, but I knew he wasn't. "They got guns out here." I said as I tucked the twenty away.

"Hell, they've got guns everywhere."

"Yeah, but here they'll kill you just for being white."

"Son, I've been all over the world and one thing I've learned, if you treat people with respect you usually don't have too many problems."

"You married?" I asked.

He nodded. "Twenty-seven years."

"How do you think your wife's gonna feel, you get yourself shot in some bar on the West Side of Chicago?"

"I'll take my chances," he said.

"And I'll wait right here."

"One drink," he said.

"Not gonna happen."

"Don't you ever get tired of being afraid?"

"Hey, fuck you, pal." There aren't five drivers in town would have even brought him out here.

"What's the worst that could happen?"

"They kill us," I said. That seemed simple enough.

"Everybody dies," he said, and I got a sudden glimpse of my

own funeral. Nobody was there. Who'd miss me besides a kid I hadn't seen in years?

I coasted a few feet to the next cross street, made a U-turn in the intersection, then pulled to the curb in front of the bar. "I'm probably going to regret this," I said.

He stuck a hand over the front seat. "Name's Floyd," he said with a smile.

"Eddie," I said, shaking his hand. "Make sure that door's locked, okay?"

Floyd led the way. It was strange being on the sidewalk in a neighborhood as decrepit as this. For years, I'd been getting out in bad neighborhoods to open the trunk or to help some invalid to the door. But to actually be going up the sidewalk on the way to a West Madison saloon. If the boys could see me now, I thought, but then I realized there was no way I could ever tell them. They'd never let me live it down.

Floyd wasn't thinking about potential dangers. He was smiling with memories. "Used to be a used car lot here." He gestured towards the weed- and junk-filled corner next to the bar. "Whitey's," Floyd said. "Had a thing about Fords."

"Pitched for the Yankees," I remembered.

The door was locked. Floyd peered through a small diamond-shaped window that had an iron grate on the back. "People in there," he said, and he started to knock. Amber bar light glowed through hazy Plexiglas.

"Closing time," I said. I started back for the cab, and he could forget about ever seeing that twenty again.

"Open up," Floyd shouted, and knocked a little harder.

"Take it easy," I said. You could get killed pounding on doors in this part of town. A buzzer sounded and Floyd pushed the door. I turned and followed him inside.

It was just a small neighborhood place. We could have been

anywhere in town. The lighting was low, mostly from assorted beer signs, some brands long out of business. There was a bar along one wall with a curve by the front. The stools were mismatched. Some had backs but most didn't. They were covered in red or black vinyl. A row of three-sided booths was covered in red. A silent jukebox, with tiny Italian lights flashing to some unheard beat, stood against the back wall.

Three guys sitting around the curve swiveled on their stools to watch us enter. They were all black, of course. The oldest was probably pushing sixty. His hair was turning grey. He watched us through tiny, octagon-shaped glasses. I could see him back in the Sixties, wearing a beret with his fist in the air.

The others were probably a decade or two younger. They were both wearing CTA bus driver uniforms but neither drove the Happy Bus. There was a TV playing above their head, some old black and white, the sound down low.

The bartender was a kid in his twenties, tall and thin, with a tiny beard, bushy eyebrows, and a neat afro. He was dressed up like an old-time bartender: rolled sleeves, a black vest, white apron.

There was only one other customer, a small guy sitting all alone at the far end of the bar staring into his drink. From the looks of it, that was all the company he'd ever need.

The bartender watched us approach. He drummed his fingers on the bar. He looked to his right. He looked to his left.

"Evening," Floyd said.

"The boss'll be right down," the bartender said nervously. And there was the sound of someone hurrying down a staircase.

"Don't need the boss," Floyd said. "Just some Tennessee whiskey." He moved a couple of stools out of the way and staked out a position in the center of the bar. "Call yours," he said to me.

"Beer," I decided.

A door behind the bar opened. "Fellows, fellows," the boss appeared. "What seems to be the problem?" He was a short black guy, about Floyd's age. He had a healthy potbelly and a shiny bald head. He wore a white dress shirt, the tails exposed.

"No problem," Floyd said. "Just stopped for a drink."

"A drink?" the boss said. "Sure, Sure," he gestured towards the bartender who hadn't made any move to fill our order. "Not too often we get the pleasure of serving the department. What'll it be, gentlemen?"

Floyd shook his head. "We're not with any department."

The boss looked towards the bartender. The bartender shrugged.

One of the bus drivers slipped off his stool and looked out the front window. "Sky Blue Cab," he announced.

"I used to drink in here years ago," Floyd explained, and the more he talked the sillier it sounded. "Thought I'd stop by and see what the old neighborhood looked like."

The boss started to laugh. "Oh, goddamn," he said, like it was the funniest thing he'd heard in weeks. "Get these boys a drink. Service!" he shouted, and laughed some more. The bus drivers and the old-timer joined in the laughter.

Floyd glanced my way, a worried look on his face. I shook my head. This hadn't been my idea.

"You had that big old Oldsmobile, didn't you?" the boss asked.

"That's right." Floyd smiled then peered at the boss. "Do I know you?"

"Oh, that was some beautiful car," the boss said and then he spoke to the bar at large, "Two-tone, white and lavender. Name's Mitchell," he said extending his hand. "This is my place."

"You didn't own it back then," Floyd said as they shook hands.

"Oh, hell no." Mitchell laughed. "I was just some kid worked in the car wash. But the day I saw that For Sale sign under my own name, I knew this place was meant for me."

"Goddamn," Floyd suddenly remembered. "You worked at the gas station."

"That's right," Mitchell said, and he smiled back. "This was some beautiful neighborhood, way back when."

"The best," Floyd said. "Do you remember…"

And that was it. They were off to the races. One story followed another and the drinks began to flow.

After a while one of the bus drivers carried his drink over and set it down next to me. "How long you been pushing a hack?" he asked.

"Long enough to know better."

"I drove for Yellow for eight years, until I got wise and switched over." He pointed to his bus driver's badge. "Name's Ron."

"Eddie," I said.

Ron lowered his voice. "How much you get, bring this boy out here?"

"Thirty so far and the meter's still running."

He showed me all his teeth, gleaming white, in a big smile. "That's nice," he said. "I took an old boy down to Peoria one day, waited for him to drop an envelope and came right back. Four hundred dollars."

"I never get those." I shook my head.

"Another time I took a whole load of people up to Wisconsin in the middle of a blizzard, couldn't see the goddamn road half the time. Nobody out but some trucks and me. I came back with over six hundred but it took me damn near two days."

"Nice," I said.

"I sort of question your judgment, walking in here."

"I question it myself," I agreed.

"I figure that's a piece in your pocket."

I shrugged. It was the mace. But if it looked like a gun, so much the better.

"I keep a .22 in the transfer pouch. Someday one of these punks is gonna make me use it and I'll be back driving the cab."

The bartender turned down the lights and slipped on a jacket. "See you tomorrow, Mitch," he said as he headed for the front door.

"Is it that late already?" Mitchell asked, and he turned to look at a clock which read 2:15. It was 2 A.M., real time. He took a look down the bar. All the customers were still in place. He lifted his arm and started to say something to the fleeing bartender, then changed his mind. "Oh, what the hell," he said. "Who's ready?"

Everybody was. I switched to bourbon. "On the house," Mitchell said. He took the same bottle down to the far end of the bar and poured into the glass sitting in front of the small man. "You're gonna drink yourself to death, Red," he said. "Then where am I gonna be?"

The man didn't say anything. He lifted the drink to his lips but his eyes stayed down.

"I used to come out this way too," Ron said a drink or so later. "Madison Street. Roosevelt Road. Pulaski. Cicero. Chicago Avenue. Hell, I used to cruise 16th Street sometimes."

"You're braver than me."

"But then I moved up north with everybody else. Lincoln Park. The Gold Coast. All those beautiful people. All them cabs, like rats in a maze. Yeah the money was better. Safer. But then I found myself passing up my own people, telling 'em I don't go south, I don't go west. My own people, man. Yeah, thought I was white there for a while but then I got wise to myself and I came back out here. And then I'd pick up anybody.

I mean anybody. But it got to be too much. Got so I couldn't stand the blood."

"Blood?"

"What do you do if someone sticks a gun in your head?"

I shrugged. It had only happened once. But I'd given them the money. What else could you do?

"You gotta remember, a car's a weapon," Ron had the answer. "Work them pedals. Brake as hard as you can and when they come flying, boom. Then hit the gas and do it again. Bam. Get yourself a little old club. That's what I had. Wop. This one kid, every time he comes flying I smacked him. Bam. He keeps saying something but I can't figure out what. Wap. Finally, he's down on the floor. I'm over the seat bopping him on the head. Little bitty gun comes flying up. 'Toy.' I finally hear what he's been saying. 'It's a toy.' Little toy gun. 'I was only fooling.' "

"No way for you to know it was a toy."

"Big kid, but I'll bet he wasn't fifteen. Yeah, he was just fooling. Uh huh. I beat him right out of the cab, Fifth Avenue and Kostner. 'I can't see. I can't see,' he's crying. He's covered with blood, begging me to take him to the hospital. I left him there on his knees, middle of the night. Freezing fuckin' cold out." He took a sip of his beer. "Spent a couple hours cleaning up the cab and that was my last night. Stupid fucking kid."

"Hey, you did what…"

Ron held up his hand, then gestured down the bar.

"She was just a little slip of a thing," Floyd was telling Mitchell. "Red hair and tiny little freckles. She had this walk, I swear to god, I'd know it was her a mile away."

"Wish I could help you out," Mitchell said. "But I don't remember any Brenda. Hell, I was only in this place twice before I owned it. Day I saw the For Sale sign, and the day me and old man Mitchell signed the papers. I never missed a payment."

"Knew it had to be a woman," Ron whispered.

At 4 A.M. Mitchell shut the party down. "Sorry, boys, I hate to do it, but I've got to open in a couple of hours."

Everybody else staggered out, then Mitchell walked us to the door. "You ever back in town," he told Floyd, "stop by."

"I'll bring the family." Floyd went along with the gag.

"That'd be something," Mitchell said, and he followed us outside. "I used to talk about having a reunion for all the old timers." He gestured at the wasteland around us. "I guess it's just as well."

"If you ever hear from Brenda," Floyd said.

Mitchell shook his head and smiled. "I gotta give you credit for trying." He waved and walked back inside.

A moment later there was a loud clatter as a metal door began to descend. Within seconds, the entire storefront disappeared behind it.

We staggered out to the cab.

"You want me to drive?" Floyd offered.

"I'm fine," I said. Finer than Floyd by a mile.

The meter was at $47.60. "I'll be a son of a bitch," Floyd whispered. "You left the meter running."

"Wasn't my idea to go inside," I explained as I cranked the starter.

"Eddie, my boy," he mumbled, "I do believe I've been taken for a ride." And he fell fast asleep.

I drove through the ruins for a few blocks, then took the highway back towards the Loop. This was the best way to see the West Side, out in the left lane at 65 mph.

You could see St. Lucy's coming a long way before you actually got there. The place was spread over several city blocks, a group of tall, jazzy buildings surrounding the original hospital, a small red brick structure.

Even in the middle of the night there were plenty of lights burning. As I got closer, I tried to guess Relita's window. Was that Intensive Care up there, that block of lights on the top corner of one of the new buildings? Or was that Relita's room over there, that single lit window, surrounded by the darkness of the old building? Had they moved her there to die?

I searched for some sign but nothing came. Floyd snored softly.

A horn blared and a *Tribune* truck shot past. I looked down. Christ, I was doing 35 in the fast lane. I stepped on the gas and drifted right.

Floyd slept all the way to the hotel and woke up muttering about being taken for a ride. The meter was a few bucks shy of $60.00 and I got three crisp twenty dollar bills.

"Worth every penny, Eddie. You're a hell of a man," he said as he worked his way out of the cab. "Hell of a man."

I found myself on North Avenue cruising the strip Relita had worked. The big hooker from last night was nowhere around. I drove past her spot and then over the river. As a consolation prize, a woman standing in front of the deserted Procter & Gamble plant lifted her short skirt and gave me a free show. Behind her a sign read, AVAILABLE 15 ACRES, WILL DIVIDE. In the parking lot, weeds had started to grow through cracks in the pavement.

I don't know what I was looking for but I turned around in the mouth of Noble Street, made another pass and found more of the same.

As I slowed for the light at Clybourn Avenue, almost two blocks past the end of the strip, a young girl got off a bench. She was dressed in jeans and a powder blue jacket. Her hair was in pigtails with tiny blue ribbons dangling from the ends. She looked past me up the street, waiting for the bus, I thought, a straight kid on her way to work, with her hands pushed deep in her jacket pockets to guard against the cold. And just being normal she was ten times better looking than any of the trash I'd just seen.

The girl did a little step and spun all the way around, and if she didn't have my attention before she had it now. She shrugged slightly, with her hands still in her pockets and her jacket opened just a touch.

Her breasts were small and rounded. They seemed lighter than the surrounding skin, almost yellow, I thought, but maybe that was the glow of the street lights. Her nipples were hidden just beyond the edge of the jacket and I was almost ready to pay to see them. It was that nice a tease.

She closed the jacket and I looked up, and she smiled and blew me a kiss.

She was just another whore out on the street at five in the morning, waiting to fuck or suck whoever came along with a few dollars for her time. But she was still subtle enough, or fresh enough, that she was also just a kid in jeans and sneakers. And if she had nothing under her jacket, that only made me want her a little more; like I might want any good looking woman after catching a glimmer of forbidden skin.

It was just a passing fancy, a pleasant little red-light dream. I doubt I would have ever followed through.

A horn sounded and I looked up to find the light green. I took my foot off the brake, waved goodbye and drove away smiling.

I pulled into the left-turn lane at Halsted and looked back in the mirror. A van had pulled to the curb and the girl was leaning in the passenger window, casting a lean profile in my mirror.

I waited for a car to clear, then made the turn and headed north.

Maybe if I hadn't been drinking it wouldn't have taken so long to register. As it was, I was almost a mile away before it hit me. I made a U-turn and sped back, but the van and the girl were both gone.

❖

At home, I poured bourbon on ice and carried the phone to the window.

Hagarty and Casper were on the street, a sergeant told me. He took my name and number and a few minutes later the phone rang. "Eddie, don't you ever sleep?" Hagarty asked.

"Pretty soon," I said. "Look, I was down on North Avenue a while ago and there was this van down there, you know, talking to one of the girls."

"You get the plate number?"

"See, that's the thing," I explained, "I didn't get anything. I didn't really realize what I saw till a few blocks later, and then when I went back they were gone."

"You're sure it was the same van?"

"Not really," I had to admit.

"What'd the driver look like?"

"I never saw him."

"Eddie, you been drinking?"

"What's that got to do with anything?"

"Have a couple more and call me tomorrow."

I sat there sipping my drink, looking out the window. It was a grey, misty morning. The day people were waiting down at the bus stop, a line of ghosts trying to escape on the CTA.

Betty knocked on her way out, but I just sat at the window and watched as she joined the crowd.

I sat there for hours, sipping whiskey. Long after Betty's bus had come and gone it began to rain. Lenny's funeral was at ten, but the hour came and went and I was still watching traffic pass.

Sometime later I picked up the phone and dialed. My ex would be at work, my daughter still at school. I was expecting a recorded message but not the one I got.

"The number you are calling has been disconnected," a mechanical voice said, and repeated the number I'd been dialing for years. "No further information is available about..." The voice repeated the number again.

In my dreams I worked without a cab, carrying passengers on my shoulders. My daughter flagged me. She was still a little girl. She had many suitcases and I kept trying to rearrange them so I could carry them all. Then it wasn't my daughter. It was Relita. No. It was the girl who had done the dance on North Avenue. She smiled as I unzipped her jacket. Her breasts were small and chocolate brown, the nipples a bright, strawberry red.

I lifted her up, breast to my mouth. "I give good head," she whispered in my ear.

"This is all I want," I said, and I tried to hold on but she pulled away and her mouth began to move down my chest.

No vehicle licensed by the City of Chicago shall be operated to solicit or accept passengers unless it is in a clean condition. Minimum standards of cleanliness include, but are not limited to:

i. The interior of the vehicle (including the trunk) shall be kept free from all waste paper, cans, garbage, or any other item not intrinsic to the vehicle or to the conduct of operating a public passenger vehicle;

ii. The interior of the vehicle (including the trunk) shall be kept free from all dirt, grease, oil, adhesive resin, or any other item which can be transferred onto the person, clothing or possessions of a passenger by incidental contact;

iii. The interior of the vehicle shall be kept free of any material which a reasonable person would find noxious or unpleasant.

City of Chicago, Department of Consumer Services,
Public Vehicle Operations Division

I was downstairs waiting when my dayman Irv pulled up about ten minutes after six. He was almost seventy years old. His face had lost most of its color and his eyes seemed to recede more each day, but his hair was still a thick, wavy brown, and he still managed to drive six days a week. He took every Sunday off and I kept the cab straight through from Saturday night until Monday morning.

"Sorry I'm late," he said as I slid into the back seat.

"No problem," I said. The rain was still falling, the sky grey. "How's business?"

"Nothing but money," he said, "but Jesus, traffic's a bitch." He turned right on Montrose into a sea of red brake lights.

"I think I'll go hide," I said.

"Eddie, you've got to get it while it's hot."

"I hate driving in the rain," I said.

"You hear about the blockade?" he asked.

"What blockade?"

"Bunch of dot-heads blocked LaSalle in front of City Hall. Fucked up the whole Loop."

"You're kidding."

He shook his head. "They had to pick a Friday."

"What was it this time?"

"Bulletproof shields. What else?"

I didn't say anything for a while, then I blurted it out. "I wonder what Lenny would say."

He put his arm up on the back of the seat. "Look, Eddie, I know the Polack was your friend but that doesn't change a fucking thing. A shield's only gonna protect you from somebody you shouldn't have picked up in the first place."

"I guess you're right," I said.

"Hell, I know I am," Irv said. "Remember I drove with one for five years. Worst years I ever had and I got robbed twice."

I grunted. I'd heard the stories before.

"It just changes the game around. They try to con you out of the cab. You never saw so many people lugging those cheap cardboard suitcases around."

"I've been having a bad week," I confessed.

"Yeah, I noticed," Irv agreed as he turned down his own block. "You forgot the ashtrays this morning."

"Sorry," I said.

He double-parked and grabbed his bag. "Don't let 'em get you down," he said, and sprinted for home.

I got behind the wheel, slid my chauffeur's license into the holder, the mace into the ashtray.

I made a left at Irving Park and joined the traffic waiting for the light at Ashland.

There was a van about ten cars up with a chrome ladder on the back door. I fashioned a third lane a couple inches off the parked cars and crept forward.

The van was too dark, I saw as I got closer. There was a bumper sticker on the back but it was on the wrong door and backed in white. IF THIS VAN'S A ROCKIN', it read, DON'T COME A KNOCKIN'.

Even in the grey rain, St. Lucy's looked like some city of the future. Gleaming glass-and-steel walkways linked the various buildings a few stories above street level.

I parked at the back of an empty cab stand, walked up a ramp and pushed through a revolving door.

ALL VISITORS MUST CHECK IN, a sign read. I leaned on a counter and waited until an older woman with frosted blue hair got off the phone. A name tag identified her as a volunteer. "May I help you?" she asked.

"I want to visit Relita Brown."

"Do you know the room number?"

"She's supposed to be in Intensive Care."

The woman flipped through a file. "Well, here's some good news," she said. "It looks like your friend's gotten better. She's been transferred to a regular floor." She started through another file, handed me a cardboard Visitor Pass, and pointed the way to the elevators.

Upstairs, I walked past the nurse's station, then stuck my head in the second door on the right. There was a woman sitting in a chair reading a book. She looked to be about thirty, slim and very black. She was wearing a pink robe and matching slippers. After a moment she looked up.

"I must have the wrong room," I said. She was the only one around.

"Who are you looking for?"

"Relita Brown."

The woman raised a finger into the air. "Leta," she called.

Now I saw that there was a second bed beyond a long white curtain. I could see the foot of the bed just where the curtain stopped.

The woman walked to the curtain. "Leta," she said again. I didn't hear any answer but after a moment she waved me over. "It's okay," she said.

I walked past her to the foot of the bed. Relita was lying on her side, facing a window that looked out on the city. She was wearing a thin white hospital gown and was curled up on top of tangled sheets. She looked even smaller than she had in the alley.

The top of the gown opened down the back and I could see thick white bandages against dark brown skin. Everything in the room was white except her skin and a small yellow radio lying next to her on the bed. A set of headphones dangled from it and I could hear music; a pounding beat, muted and far away.

"Hi," I said. But she didn't answer or turn my way.

I walked around the bed to the window side. She didn't look up. The side of her face was bruised and swollen. Her head lay on a pillow. Both hands were tucked up under her chin, her wrists crossed.

She didn't look anything like the girl I'd seen on North Avenue last night, the girl with the pigtails, the girl of my dreams. There wasn't an ounce of sexiness about Relita and it was hard to imagine that anyone had ever paid for her company. She was just an injured animal waiting to die. A small, dark animal that someone had dressed as a gag.

"Hi," I said. "It's Eddie Miles. Remember me?"

"Eddie," she said softly. She tilted her head my way but her eyes didn't quite make the trip. They were off somewhere, hidden behind bleak clouds.

A hand reached out, balled into a tiny fist. I took it, closed my hands around it and the fist disappeared inside.

I looked up and the roommate was standing just beyond the curtain. She didn't have any problem making eye contact. She nodded her head, as if I'd just confirmed her darkest thoughts, turned and walked away.

"How're you doing?" I asked after a moment.

"Okay." Her voice was so far away, so tired, that I could never imagine her lifting her head off the pillow.

"I was in the neighborhood," I said, "so I thought, what the heck."

"Relita's angel," she whispered.

"The police told me you were here," I said.

"Don't be talking 'bout no police," she said with some force.

Nobody said anything for a while. Her eyes shifted around but never settled. They were off to one side or the other, up or down, but never dead ahead. "Maybe we mets a different way," she said after several minutes had gone by.

"Sure," I said, willing to play along. "How?"

"Slide the chair," she said.

There was a chair near the foot of the bed. I released her hand and then moved the chair alongside and sat down.

Both hands came out now and I took them and closed them up in my own. "You be my angel," she whispered.

"Sure," I said.

We sat like that for several minutes. Neither one of us said a word. Her eyes continued to shift but they never seemed to focus. They might as well have belonged to some blind man begging on a street corner. They might as well have been closed.

She was just a kid. It was hard to believe she was seventeen. She wasn't any bigger than my daughter had been the last time I'd seen her, and my daughter had only been eight years old. At the most, Relita weighed eighty pounds.

She must have grown up on a diet of potato chips and junk food, drugs and late hours, cigarettes and booze, and high-volume street sex, night after night after night.

Did she have a real lover somewhere? Maybe she had a pimp. Had he come to visit?

It suddenly hit me that Relita had become a whore when she was younger than my daughter was now.

Laura had still sounded like a little girl on the phone, but what did I know? I'd let my ex take her away and now I was a father in name only. I hadn't seen her in seven years, almost half her life, and I'd agreed not to see her for another six, until she turned twenty-one.

That would be thirteen years with no contact. Would she even remember me? Would she hate me? Would she even care? I would be out there like Floyd looking for his Brenda, thirty years after the last dance.

After a while Relita's eyes closed completely and her breathing quieted. I touched her gently on the shoulder. "Take care of yourself, kid," I said, and I released her hands and she tucked them back under her chin, moved around a bit and set-tled into position.

I stood up and looked out the window.

From twelve stories up it was easy to be fooled by the city's rain-swept beauty, by the millions of lights twinkling in the night. But all I had to do was turn my head to see the truth: a child-whore asleep in her hospital bed. It could rain forever and the city would never be clean.

Outside in the hall the roommate was waiting along with a

young white woman dressed in a dark blue business suit. The woman held a clipboard in one hand and a pen in the other. "Could I see some identification, please?" she asked, the pen ready to write.

"Huh?"

"I need your name," she said. She was wearing a name tag which identified her as Dr. Margaret Gallos.

"What for?"

"We have to have the names of anyone visiting a minor."

"I just stopped to say hello."

"She doesn't need you taking advantage of her," the room-mate said loudly.

"What's that supposed to mean?" I asked.

"Didn't you get enough already?" she shouted.

"You don't know nothing, lady," I said as I walked around them. "If it wasn't for me she'd probably be dead."

Gallos hurried after me. "You're the cabdriver, aren't you?"

"What if I am?" I asked, and I kept walking.

She followed along. "Look, I apologize for jumping to con-clusions. I'm Dr. Gallos. I've been assigned to work with Relita but it's been extremely difficult. She's very averse to talking about her ordeal. She's very averse to talking about anything, actually. But she did mention you." Gallos caught up with me and walked alongside. "Would you please stop and talk to me?"

I kept going, then stopped by the elevators and pushed the down button.

"I'm a psychologist," Gallos continued. "We have a program here to help victims of violence. It's just a pilot program right now, but we're trying. We're trying to help. Relita thinks you're quite special. It might be beneficial if you continued to visit."

"Lady, let me ask you something," I said and turned to face her. "Do I look like any kind of angel?"

"It doesn't matter what you look like to me."

A bell chimed as an elevator arrived. I stepped aboard.

"The last thing I want to do is chase you away."

I didn't answer and the door began to close.

"What have you got to lose?" Gallos asked. The door closed and I rode non-stop to the lobby.

I spent the next several hours fighting heavy traffic—the wipers beating away, the defroster barely staying ahead of the fog—listening to a string of gloomy passengers complain about the weather.

"Driver, is this rain ever going to stop?"

"Lady, if I could predict the weather, you think I'd be driving a cab for a living?"

I'd never noticed how many vans there were. And most of them seemed to have bumper stickers. I BRAKE FOR ANIMALS. I BRAKE FOR GARAGE SALES. HONK IF YOU LOVE JESUS. HONK IF YOU ARE JESUS. TRUST JESUS. TRUST JESUS BUT CUT THE CARDS.

WYOMING. HOLY HILL. WALL DRUGS.

I'D RATHER BE SAILING. FLYING. DRINKING. FISHING.

SO MANY PEDESTRIANS/SO LITTLE TIME. IF YOU DON'T LIKE THE WAY I DRIVE STAY OFF THE SIDE-WALK. I LOVE SOBER DRIVERS. HIT ME—I NEED THE MONEY.

MY CHILD IS AN HONOR STUDENT. MY KID CAN BEAT UP YOUR HONOR STUDENT. MY CHILD WAS INMATE OF THE MONTH AT COOK COUNTY JAIL. And on and on and on.

There were bumper stickers for radio stations, sports teams and political candidates. But I couldn't find the right combination; a yellow-backed sticker on the left door and a chrome ladder on the right.

Twice I made U-turns to check out vans heading in the opposite direction, and both times I turned back around.

"Driver, where the hell are you going?"

"Sorry, forgot you were back there."

I went down North Avenue. There weren't any girls around. It was just an ordinary, industrial street, shutting down for the night.

I went over the river and then stopped for the light at Clybourn. I was in the same spot as the night before, but the girl was nowhere around. There was no shelter at the bus stop, just a lopsided advertising bench, exposed to the rain.

I AM THE RESURRECTION AND THE LIFE, the bench proclaimed in faded letters. AND WHOEVER BELIEVES IN ME WILL NEVER DIE.

The rain finally stopped about nine o'clock. A few minutes later, an older guy in a tweed topcoat opened the door and held up a smoldering cigar. "Can I smoke this thing in there?"

"Sure," I said, and he slid in. "Where to?"

"You know Pelly's?"

"On Irving Park?"

"That's the place." He slurred the words.

Yeah, I knew Pelly's, a dark steakhouse–piano bar miles off the beaten path.

Once upon a time it had been our favorite spot. Our first visit had been one of those nights you always remember. After we married it became our special place. We'd gone there for just about every anniversary, every birthday, any romantic occasion.

But our last visit had been one of those nights you try not to remember. It was the night I got the first hint of where we were heading, the beginning of the end. And I hadn't been inside since.

My passenger seemed lost in thought as we headed north-west. The sweet smell of the cigar filled the cab and, for the first time in years, I remembered some of the good times we'd had.

"This place still good?" I asked as we pulled in front.

"Wonderful joint," the guy said, handing me a twenty. "Been coming here for years."

"I used to come myself," I said.

"Remember Clifford?" The guy leaned over the front seat. The scent of cognac mingled with the cigar smoke.

"Who's that?"

"Big, tall kid, used to be bartender."

"That rings a bell," I lied. The truth was, I'd spent very little time at the bar.

They'd had several private booths back then. It was a great place to hold hands and look into each other's eyes—or do whatever the hell you wanted. You could sit at the bar any-where in town. This was the place for romance.

"My son-in-law," the guy said sadly. "He broke my heart, that kid. But I'd still love him. Swear to god, I'd still love him."

I handed him his change and he dropped a five over the front seat. "Where's Clifford when I need him?" he asked the waiting doorman.

"Clifford?" the doorman said. "Clifford's been gone for years." He closed my door then hurried ahead and opened the door to Pelly's. A piano was playing softly, red lights flickered in a warm, enticing glow.

I sat there a moment, memories swirling in the cigar smoke, torn between remembering and forgetting.

The doorman walked around to my window. He was an older black guy, and he'd been at Pelly's as long as I could remember; parking cars, opening doors and witnessing enough scenes and bitter words that I was sure ours were long forgotten. "If you wanna wait, do me a favor and back it up a bit," he said. "They'll probably... Hey, where you been? I ain't seen you in years."

"Yeah," I said, "I don't get around much anymore."

He snapped his fingers, pointed, and sang: "Missed the Saturday dance..." He had the song down cold. I took my foot off the brake, waved, and left him singing.

I drove a few blocks, then turned on Avondale without really thinking, following the old route home.

"Yo!" I was sitting at a red light on Pulaski, still lost in a daydream, when I looked up to find two kids heading straight for my cab.

They were probably in their mid-teens. One was black and one was Puerto Rican. My immediate reaction was to just get the hell out of there. But then I decided, they weren't quite red-light-running material.

The Puerto Rican was tall and skinny, wearing one of those hooded sports jackets with the hood down. The black kid was a little fire hydrant of a guy. He was wearing dark, baggy pants, belted tight about four inches below his waist. How could a kid who looked so funny be dangerous?

"Can you take us to Armitage?" the black kid asked as they climbed in.

"And then what?" I asked.

"Central Park, right by the corner, okay?" the same kid asked nervously.

"Sure," I said, and I hit the meter and started away.

"It's already a dollar twenty," the Puerto Rican said. He sounded shocked.

"Plus that fifty cents," the black kid pointed out the extra passenger charge.

"Motherfucker was cold," the Puerto Rican said.

"He was just playing with you, man," the black kid said.

I looked in the mirror and they'd both disappeared. "Hey, what the fuck's going on?" I turned around and they were slouched as low as you could go, their heads way below the window line.

"Hey, we're cool, man." The black kid held up two empty hands. "We're cool."

"What's going on?" I asked again.

"Nothing man," the Puerto Rican mumbled. "Why's everybody fucking with us?"

"Hey, man, there ain't nobody following us, is there?" the black kid asked.

I checked the mirror and there were two cars behind us. They weren't too close but they weren't very far either. I pulled to the side and let them pass.

"What you doin', man?"

"I ain't gettin' in the middle of your shit," I said as I sped up.

"We got money," the Puerto Rican said.

"There ain't no yellow Toyota back there, is there?" the black kid asked.

I shook my head.

"See, we was waitin' for the bus," the black kid explained, "and this gangster dude drives by real slow, and then backs up. 'I like your jacket,' he tells my friend. You sure there ain't nobody back there?"

"I'll let you know if I see any yellow cars," I said. "In the meantime, you guys mind sittin' up just a little?"

They humored me for a few blocks, then crouched low again.

The street curved and went under a railroad viaduct. I turned left at Armitage and drove through a dark factory stretch and then under another viaduct.

"See, you can't own nothing good," the Puerto Rican whined.

"They stole my bike. They busted up my radio. Now they after my jacket."

"Just don't flash it at night," the black kid advised. "It be too much these motherfuckers see you struttin' at night."

There was $5.30 on the meter when we pulled up at Central Park, a dim little intersection with an old public school on one corner and a vacant lot on another. The kids stayed crouched down while they dug through their pockets and found three singles each. I handed back the change, and they opened the door and ran north up the side street.

I continued east through an old Puerto Rican nightlife strip. But the bright lights, the huge signs, and the loud music were all long gone.

In Bucktown, I found a trio of drunks, two girls and a guy. They'd obviously been drinking for hours.

"Where're we going next?" one of the girls shouted in my ear.

"I gotta go home," the guy said climbing in. "I'm gonna pass out."

"Come on," both girls screamed.

I started the meter. Sometimes those little red numbers helped people decide.

"Elm and Dearborn," the guy said, and he closed his eyes.

"What a spoilsport," one of the girls said as I headed for the highway.

I was on Division Street when one of the girls said, "Is this Cabrini-Green?"

"Why are you taking us this way?" the other girl asked. "You want us to get shot or something?"

"I would have taken you the long way if you'd asked."

"How'd you like to break down around here?" the guy woke up. "Excuse me, Mr. Black Man, I'm a simple white boy from the suburbs. I wonder if you could help me?"

"Yeah, right," one of the girls agreed. "Are we really going home?"

"Just a quick nap," the guy said.

The girls groaned. "What a party pooper," one said. "Oh, well, we'll just have to entertain each other."

"Come on. Knock it off," the guy said a moment later.

I looked back in the mirror. The girls were kissing.

"Don't do that," the guy shouted.

"Oh, you love it," one girl said. "You love watching us."

"You love it. You love it. You love it," the other girl chanted.

"You know what's funny?" the first girl asked. "Girls think two guys doing it is gross. But guys love two girls doing it. Why is that?"

"Because the guys really do it," the guy said as I pulled to the curb on Dearborn. "They don't just tease all the time."

"Yeah, wait'll we get upstairs," the first girl said. "We'll show you."

"Yeah," the other girl agreed. "Hey, Mr. Cabdriver, you want to come watch?"

The guy handed me a ten and a single. "They're just teases," he said.

"Did you see his face?" one of the girls screamed out on the sidewalk. "He would have watched all night."

Taxicab chauffeurs shall not ask the passenger his destination prior to the passenger being seated in the vehicle of which the chauffeur has charge.

City of Chicago, Department of Consumer Services,
Public Vehicle Operations Division

I was a few blocks north of Greek Town when a black girl in a shiny down jacket waved.

"Where to?" I asked as she slid in.

"Ogden and Washington," she said.

She was in her late teens or early twenties, a big girl, wearing nice tight jeans. Her hair had been dyed, not quite as red as the jacket.

"You get high?" she asked as we headed west on Madison, through the old Skid Row.

"Not while I'm working," I said.

"I got some good reefer," she said.

"Sorry," I said. "Not tonight."

"You wanna buy some food stamps?"

"I'll pass," I said.

"They're just like money," she explained. "You just take 'em to the store. I got seventy dollars here. You can have 'em for thirty-five."

"Sorry," I said again.

"Twenty for ten," she said.

"Lady, I don't want any food stamps. Okay?"

Coming up to Ogden Avenue I drifted right. There was a

hotel just off the corner at Washington and Ogden and I assumed that's where she was heading.

"You gotta turn left," she said.

"It's to the right," I told her.

"Washtenaw and Ogden," she said, and she managed this phony little giggle. "You thought I said Washington, didn't you?"

I should have thrown her out right there, or made a U-turn and taken her back to where I'd picked her up. I knew damn well she'd said Washington.

"I ain't going into no projects," I said.

"You just drop me right there on the corner," she said.

So I made the left and headed southwest towards Washtenaw, a couple of miles away. She'd conned me and now, like a chump, I was letting her get away with it.

We passed a block west of St. Lucy's. Was Relita still sleeping? I wondered what her dreams were like. I wondered if she would ever find the strength to lift her head.

There was a pair of dark low-rises off to the right at Washtenaw and Ogden. WELCOME TO OGDEN COURTS, a sign read. "Pull right behind that car," the girl said.

There was no way I was stopping behind any parked cars. "Six-eighty," I said as I turned into a local lane off the side of the main road. There was no one around. A block down a sign read EMERGENCY ROOM. Beyond the hospital was the darkness of Douglas Park.

"I gotta run upstairs and get the money," she said. "Just park right over there."

"Shit," I said. I stopped right in the middle of the lane. "You know you should have told me you didn't have money," I shouted, but I was mainly pissed at myself. I'd been a fool not to get some money the moment she'd switched destinations. I'd been a fool not to throw her out of the cab.

"I'll be right back," she said, and reached for the door. "I'm just going to the second floor."

"Leave the jacket," I said.

"I ain't leaving no two hundred dollar jacket in your cab," she said, her voice rising. She tried the door handle but that didn't get her anywhere. I was holding the door lock switch.

"Give me those food stamps you were talking about," I suggested.

"I'll pay you with food stamps," she said, and she reached into a jacket pocket. "That's cool."

"I'll hold the food stamps. You get the money."

"Here's ten," she said and she handed me one book.

"One more," I said.

"It's only six dollars," she said.

"Seven," I said. The meter had already turned.

"You got ten," she said.

"Police station's right around the corner," I warned her, and I took my foot off the brake and started to roll.

"Twenty," she said. She handed me another book and reached for the door and I popped the locks. "I be right down," she said, and hurried away. I locked the doors.

The meter turned twenty cents a minute, inching along at twelve bucks an hour. I sat there with my foot on the brake, thinking what a chump I'd been, falling for her bullshit. I was a fool for hanging around. Take the stamps and go, I told myself. It didn't make any difference if they were good or not. Every click of the meter was just a little more wasted time and another minute of possible danger. I kept checking the mirrors and looking around to make sure no one snuck up on the cab. But the place was just like Cabrini. There was no one around. All the decent folks were hiding in their apartments, and it was still a bit early for the drug dealers and thugs.

Tony Golden had once argued that cabdrivers got a lop-sided view of the poor. If you were poor and you were honest, you couldn't afford to take taxis. So many of the people who ended up in cabs in poor neighborhoods were thieves, drug dealers and other small-time hustlers. Meanwhile, the working stiffs and the welfare moms with varicose veins, three kids, and seven bags of groceries, were pushing shopping carts or struggling on the CTA.

I wondered what my passenger's hustle was. Food stamps and marijuana both seemed to be sidelines.

The meter was at seven-eighty when the girl finally returned. A big guy tagged along behind. He was twenty-five or so, wearing a T-shirt under a well-worn leather jacket. I could tell, by his slow, reluctant walk, that this wasn't his idea.

She tried the back door but found it locked. "Open up," she shouted.

I cracked the window just a bit and checked the meter. "It's seven-eighty."

"Me and my brother want to go to the North Side."

I almost laughed, it was such an old line.

"I got the money," she said, and held up two ragged twenties. I shook my head again.

"Oh, man," she moaned. The brother stood back a ways. He was the kind of guy I would pick up any day of the week. A big easygoing guy who didn't want to fuck with anybody. He wanted to be back watching TV. Whatever plan they had, it was all hers.

"Seven-eighty," I said again.

She handed a twenty through the crack in the window and I slipped her the change and the food stamps.

"You're all fucked up, man, you know that?" She turned and stalked away.

After she passed, her brother gave me a little shrug. It was okay with him, the shrug seemed to say. No hard feelings.

I shrugged back. I knew it wasn't his fault. Someday we might sit around and talk about the devious ways of women. But if I'd been foolish enough to let them in the cab, he would probably have been the one holding the knife or the gun, or with his arms wrapped around my neck.

I pulled away, then made a U-turn and headed northeast. The light at Western Avenue turned yellow as I approached. I jumped on the gas, tapped the horn, and blew right through.

Once upon a time, this stretch of Ogden Avenue had been part of the legendary Route 66, from Chicago to Los Angeles and all those points in between. It had also been the main link between the West Side and Lincoln Park. But years ago the city had begun to cut the Lincoln Park section out.

It was as if some visionary traffic engineer had seen the course the city would take; that Lincoln Park would be for the rich, and the West Side for the poor, and what was the point of a street that connected the two? Now, even in the height of rush hour, there was little traffic.

I passed St. Lucy's and Madison Street. The next block was Warren Boulevard. To my left was the hotel I'd been thinking about. There was nothing at Washington and Ogden but a union hall and a park. So maybe the girl really had said Washtenaw. Maybe I was getting a little too paranoid.

The hell with that, I decided a moment later. I'd sure clocked her on that North Side routine.

I continued up Ogden, through the old Italian neighborhood around Grand Avenue—an old syndicate neighborhood undergoing gentrification—and then drove up the long, crumbling bridge that crossed over industrial Goose Island. I passed over the river, then pulled to the side above the canal and killed the lights.

I walked to the railing and looked out. The rain was gone and most of the clouds had disappeared. For the first time in days you could actually see the city.

The western edge of Cabrini was just out of reach. It was close enough that I could see the flickering lights of scattered TV's, curtains fluttering in open windows, and vague shadows beyond. For years I'd been hearing stories about snipers firing at traffic on this bridge, and I knew they had to be true. But I'd never even heard a shot from up here and I always felt safe, a sightseer several stories up, uninvolved with whatever went on below.

To my left the Edison substation whispered softly, and I had a sudden flash of Lenny, his ass on the seat and one dead eye staring at the camera. Could Rollie have actually done that? I wondered. It was hard to imagine. But someone had. Right down there, on a street crisscrossed with shadows cast by the moon.

To my right, the old towers of the Loop were bathed in soft light, the new ones topped with antennas and flashing strobes. Down below, a line of cars rumbled over the Halsted Street Bridge, heading north. The industry on Goose Island, long in decline, was silent for the night, the water in the canal dark and murky.

I stood there for a while with the city laid out before me, the lake a dark and soothing backdrop. The Gold Coast and Lincoln Park glittered in the night, a pair of dazzling stars glowing brighter each year. It was easy to overlook Cabrini. The place was about as dim as a forty watt bulb. Behind me, the West Side was even darker.

Lord, how the city had changed, I thought, and I remembered a trip over this bridge with a girl I'd dated in high school. I wondered where she was tonight.

I thought about my daughter, too. Just to hear her voice, to hear the excitement when she'd said, *Daddy, where have you been?* was almost worth losing the phone number. How would I find the new one? I didn't have an address, only the name of the town. What if they moved? I wondered if she was thinking of me right now.

I wondered about the girl last night too. Had she really gotten into that van? Did she ever get out? Christ, how could I have been so stupid?

A couple of cars went over the bridge while I stood there but that was it. There wasn't any traffic. The city had spent years making the span virtually useless and now they were on the brink of success. It was a long bridge to nowhere in desperate need of repair. But the repairs were never going to come. The city had recently announced their intentions to tear the whole thing down. Who the hell wanted to go to the West Side anyway?

I pissed between rusty iron rails, rippling the water down in the canal, then got in the cab and drove down the bridge, and then another block to Clybourn where Ogden now ended.

A few blocks ahead any hint of the old street had disappeared. The path leading through Old Town to Lincoln Park had been filled with fancy new townhouses and million-dollar single-family homes. A highrise condominium stood just west of where Ogden had once spilled into Clark Street, a little southwest of the Lincoln Park Zoo.

But you couldn't get there from the West Side. There was a barricade dead ahead. Cabrini was to my right. I turned left and headed northwest up Clybourn. I didn't feel much like working. I hadn't felt like working all night. I could have a cup of coffee with Rollie, I thought, and I remembered that he'd offered to buy.

I wondered if the police had talked to him and I felt a twinge of guilt. He had seemed like a good kid. A street smart one, granted, but that didn't make him a murderer. But if he was, he was a great con man too. He was wasting his talents robbing cabs.

A "NOT FOR HIRE" sign shall be displayed when:

1. the chauffeur is responding to radio or telephone orders;

2. the vehicle is in disrepair or out of service or the meter is out of service;

3. the chauffeur is returning to the garage;

4. the chauffeur is en route for meals or personal necessity.

City of Chicago, Department of Consumer Services,
Public Vehicle Operations Division

Rollie and Mohammed were right where I'd left them, one behind the other like some third-world comedy team.

"Look who's here," Rollie sang the moment I stepped inside.

"I thought I'd take you up on that offer."

"How's that?"

"You said you'd buy the coffee," I reminded him.

"Hey, I was hopin' you'd forget." He smiled that big, gold-tooth smile and waved me towards the coffee. "You got to pour it yourself, now."

"No problem," I said.

I walked to the back and filled a small go-cup and carried it up front. Rollie took a bill out of his wallet and held it up for Mohammed to see. "I be buying the coffee for my friend here," he explained.

I held the cup up in a toast. "Thanks," I said.

Rollie held the change out for Mohammed to see before slipping it into his pocket. "Course now real friends don't be giving their partners up to no po-lice," he said softly.

"How's that?" I said.

"Oh shit, man," he said, "I be cool but I ain't no fool. I know you put 'em on me. But hey, I been there before. Hard to be a black man in this city without the man coming down on you now and then. But you know what bothers me?" he asked as another clerk walked out from the back room.

"To be perfectly honest," I lied, "I don't know what the hell you're talking about."

"Yeah, well that's cool," he said. "I'd be perfectly honest too, I be wearing your boots. Look, do me a favor, Eddie, I got to check out. But hang around a minute. I got to ask you one little thing."

"What's that?"

"This only take a minute," he said as he pushed some buttons on the register and pulled out the cash drawer. "Why don't you get yourself a refill there, Eddie, my man. We always give free refills to our special friends. Ain't that right, Mohammed?"

Mohammed didn't say a thing. He kept his eyes glued to the register.

I walked to the back and splashed coffee in my cup, then strolled up and down the aisles wishing I'd never come.

It took him about five minutes to check out, then Rollie waved me back by the coffee and poured himself a cup. "Decaf," he explained. "I gotta get me some sleep tonight. See, last night I was sound asleep and here come the po-lice pounding on the door, waking up the whole damn house. Waking my mamma, my poor ol' mamma. You think they'd do that to some white family, Eddie, start banging on the door in the middle of the night?"

I shrugged innocently. How had I suddenly become an expert on police procedure?

"And then they all apologetic," Rollie went on. "Yeah, said

they thought we was up 'cause they saw the TV was on. Now they know damn well you turn that TV off where I live, won't be long before it be walking off down the alley. And now my mamma, she all upset and crying and carrying on. Homicide, they tell her, they want to talk to me about some homicide. I tell you, man, that woke me right up. Homicide, yeah, that opened my eyes like a shot, sit me up straight in bed. Homicide.

"But my poor mamma. I tell you, after a while I think they take more time trying to calm her down than they did talking to me. And then they say not to worry, it was just some cabdriver give 'em my name. Some clown cabdriver, man, and I knew it had to be you."

"What was this question you wanted to ask?" I said, trying to evade the issue.

"You ain't really be thinkin' I killed your friend?" Rollie looked me straight in the eyes. "That's what I want to know."

"Hey," I held my hands out wide, "I never told anybody that."

"Shit," Rollie said. "See, it really gets me, man, you or anybody else be thinking I'm some killer. Some stone killer."

"I just came in to get some coffee," I said.

"You think I look like a killer, man?"

"No," I had to admit.

"You want to take a ride down to the old hood," he offered, "I'll show you some killers. I don't think you know what a killer really look like."

"Look, if I caused you any problems, I apologize. I guess I wasn't thinking."

"That's right," Rollie said. "You just be out there runnin' your mouth like a fool, messing with people's lives."

"Sorry," I said.

He looked at me and shook his head, and then, after a while, he seemed to relax, and he showed me the gold tooth again, bright and shiny. "It's cool, Eddie," he said. "I know how it be, you lose a friend. Everything's cool."

"Thanks," I said. Rollie offered his hand and we shook, then we stood there sipping coffee, bullshitting about this and that.

Rollie was twenty-two, he told me, and he wasn't planning to spend his entire life as a convenience store clerk. He was working nights while going to school days. He was hoping to become either an insurance underwriter or an embalmer.

"An embalmer?" I asked.

"Yeah, see, I got an uncle do that. And he say I got the apti-tude. But I don't know, man," he shook his head, "I went down there one time but I don't think it's the life for me."

"Jesus, that sounds worse than driving a cab."

Rollie put a hand on my shoulder and guided me away from the coffee counter. "Gotta make room for the paying cus-tomers," he said.

"Thanks, fellows," a voice behind me said.

Rollie pulled me closer and whispered in my ear. "It's Tweety Bird."

I glanced at the guy behind us. "Who?" I whispered.

"Tweety Bird." Rollie giggled.

The new customer was a little guy in an oversized striped shirt. He had big eyes, a tiny nose, and a stomach that looked about eight months gone. He was bald except for a few strands of stray hair that floated around his head. His shoes must have been size fourteen.

I watched him pour sugar and hot chocolate mix into an extra-large commuter cup and then add coffee. I decided he could probably make a decent circus clown. All he'd need was a big light-up nose and a little paint. Maybe I'd put a little paint on myself and join him, driving a miniature taxicab.

"Who's Tweety Bird?" I asked.

"I tawt I taw a puddy tat," Rollie said, as if that explained something.

"Huh?"

"Tweety Bird and Sylvester the cat?" Rollie looked at me expectantly.

I shook my head.

"Man, weren't you ever a kid?"

We stood there a while longer, then I dropped my empty cup in the trash, and held out my hand. "Sorry again if I caused you any trouble."

"We cool, Eddie," he said, and took my hand. "We cool."

"I'll see you around." I started for the door.

"Hey, Eddie," he called after me, "can you wait a minute and give me a ride home?"

I froze. I couldn't move forward. I couldn't turn around.

A tight little laugh came from behind. "Eddie, it kind of pisses me off you ain't sure."

"Come on, Rollie." I finally managed to turn and face him. "You know better than that."

"Okay, let me just grab my things," he said. But he didn't move. He stood there watching me.

"Look, I gotta be somewhere." I shrugged in apology. "Maybe some other time."

Rollie shook his head. "Eddie, I'd love to play poker with you," he said. "Man, you'd go home without your pants. You are some terrible liar. Mohammed," he called, "this boy needs to take some lessons, learn to keep that stone face." He pointed a finger at me, a finger without a hint of friendship, then turned and walked into the back room.

Mohammed didn't say a word and his face didn't move. The new clerk watched me with little interest. He was an older black guy with wiry salt and pepper hair and thick glasses. He'd probably seen it all, working the midnight shift in an out-of-the-way convenience store on the edge of a deteriorating neighborhood.

Mohammed stood in his usual spot behind the clerk, a contemporary version of the cigar store Indian. I wondered if he ever went home.

There was a van parked next to my cab. It was rusty red with teardrop windows on the side. Tweety Bird was sitting behind the wheel.

I walked around back and there was a chrome ladder on the back. I took a few steps, to check for a bumper sticker, and a gruff voice, right at my side, whispered, "Hey, buddy, help me out." I barely managed to keep from jumping.

I took a couple of half steps instead and looked over and there was this wreck of a human. He was skinny and poor, wearing dark, tattered rags that blended into the night.

"Let me see what I got." I found some change and dropped it into his waiting hand, then headed back toward my cab.

"Man, you can do better than that," he said, following. Suddenly his voice was loud and clear.

"No, that's it," I said, and slid into the front seat, slamming the door behind me.

He mumbled something I didn't understand, turned and shuffled into the darkness.

A few minutes later, I decided I should have given him more. But by then I was already several blocks away, following the van south down Western Avenue.

The bumper sticker was in the exact right spot, three lines on a yellow background. CAUTION, it read. HORN OUT OF ORDER. PLEASE WATCH FOR FINGER.

Tweety Bird wasn't in any hurry. He stayed in the right lane. I hung back a block or more, trying to keep some cars between us. The way the van moved I could almost see him up there, sipping coffee, one hand on the wheel.

Western Avenue was supposedly the longest city street in the world. That's what the Chicago boosters said. It ran from the city limits on the north to the city limits on the south, twenty-some miles, and finally ended somewhere in the south suburbs.

Once upon a time it had been the western border of town and North Avenue had been the northern. Now the city went on forever. Western Avenue was best known for its automobile dealerships and North Avenue for its whores.

We went up the overpass over Belmont Avenue. Just to the right was Area Six. Hagarty and Casper were probably still drinking their wake-up coffee. "Come on, guys," I whispered as I passed. "Take a little ride."

I could stop and make a quick call, or declare an emergency over my two-way radio, but I'd almost be embarrassed. I'd already sicced the cops on one innocent man, I didn't want to do it again. And how could a guy who looked like Tweety Bird be a killer?

The van continued past North Avenue, which didn't surprise me. I knew I was just wasting my time.

Maybe I'd get lucky, I thought, and Tweety Bird would lead me straight out of town, to the farms and fields so far away.

But then at Lake Street the van turned east. The elevated tracks were above us. There was an industrial area on the left, and a few blocks later, housing projects on the right. It was hard to get more urban than this.

Not exactly an innocent neighborhood, I thought. Not for an older white guy. But maybe he worked in the area, I told myself. He certainly drove like a union man getting paid by the hour.

Meanwhile I wasn't making a dime following along.

He continued east in the same leisurely manner; a guy who happened to drive a van that looked like the one I'd seen. There were a million vans around town. A couple of them had to match.

He stopped for a light and there was nowhere to hide so I pulled up right behind him. A moment later the light changed and I dropped back a half-block or so, not very far in the darkness under the el. If the guy was paying attention, he knew I was there.

Past the projects there was industry on both sides of the street. The old produce market was one block south on Randolph, meat packing houses were a block north on Fulton. A train rumbled overhead, dropping sparks as it headed east.

Just beyond Morgan, the van's brake lights flashed. And then there was a black girl waving from behind a rusty girder. But he passed her by. I was about to pass, too, but then I stopped instead.

The girl walked to the passenger window as the van continued away. She was tall and well built with very light skin. She was wearing shiny short-shorts and a halter top under an open jacket. "How you doin' dear?" She leaned into the open window. There was a slight twang in her voice, just a hint of the south.

I pulled a ten dollar bill out of my pocket and held it up. "Ever see that van before?"

"He don't never stop," she said, and backed away a bit.

"But he comes by?"

"He look. He don't play." She reached for the ten but I pulled it back.

"You see him a lot?"

"He go round and round some nights."

"You sure?" I asked. A few blocks ahead, the van turned north on Halsted.

"He so dog ugly," she said, "how I not be sure?"

I handed her the ten and she slipped it into her shorts. "Don't buy nothin' but a flash and a dash," she said and lifted her halter to give me a peek, then ran into the darkness laughing.

I jumped on the gas and went after the van. It was the guy, I was sure. He'd taken the long way around but now he was heading for North Avenue. As I turned on Halsted, I flicked the two-way on. As soon as I spotted him, I would use the radio to get the police.

I shot up Halsted but I never caught up with Tweety Bird.

I turned left on Clybourn and left again on North. There were plenty of girls out, strutting their stuff down the avenue, but the van was nowhere around. I'd let him know I was following and now he was gone.

I retraced my steps back to Lake Street, and then once again to North Avenue, where I pulled into a gas station and up to the pay phone.

"Hagarty," the detective came on the line.

"It's Eddie Miles," I said. "Look, I think I saw that van again." "Where?"

I described my ride. "A girl on Lake Street told me he comes by almost every night but he doesn't stop."

"Eddie, the guy we're looking for stops."

"Maybe she isn't his type," I said.

"You get a plate number this time?" he asked, but he didn't sound very excited.

I gave him the number.

"I hope this isn't another one of those Rollie gags."

"What gag?" I said. "I didn't tell you to kick his door down."

"We'll check it out," he said. "You never know. Hey, tell me about that girl at the bus stop last night. What'd she look like?"

"She was just a kid," I remembered. "Real straight looking. Jeans. Light blue jacket. Her hair was in pigtails and she had these blue ribbons tied on the ends."

"If you're in the neighborhood later, stop by. Something I want to show you."

"Tonight?"

"No hurry," he said. "Tonight, tomorrow, whenever you get time."

There were several familiar cabs parked by the Golden Batter Pancake House. But I knew if I stopped I'd have to explain why I'd missed Lenny's funeral. I headed east and north instead.

I was drunk. Isn't that good enough?

And Lenny wouldn't be coming to mine.

On Broadway, a skinny guy in an imitation leather jacket waved. A blond girl waited on the sidewalk.

"I've only got a buck and a half," the guy said. "Can you take us up Clarendon just north of Irving for that?"

"It's only two blocks."

"My lady's got a bad leg." He shrugged and smiled.

"What the hell," I said. All I was losing was the fifty cents extra passenger charge and any tip I might get.

"Here you go, guy," he said after they crawled in, and he handed me a handful of clammy change. "Count it. There should be a buck fifty there."

"I'll take your word for it." I dumped the coins into an empty coffee cup, then wiped my hands on my pants.

"Let me ask you a question," he said. "You like pussy?"

I looked back in the mirror. They were both watching me, phony smiles planted on their faces. She was a very old twenty-five. They were both hard looking, cheap white trash.

"Can't you guys wait till you get home?"

"Hey, whatever you say," he shrugged.

Broadway curved to the west. I kept straight and went north on Clarendon, a residential through street which was the dividing line between seedy Uptown and the narrow well-to-do lakefront neighborhood to the east. There were a couple of sets of taillights a few blocks ahead. Nobody was coming our way.

Just past Irving Park I checked the rearview and the girl was turned around looking out the back window. It must be something they all learned in prison, I thought. Or maybe this was what I was missing by not watching prime time TV. I grabbed the can of mace and set it on my lap.

"Turn left," the guy said.

The next street was narrow and only ran one block to Broadway. There was a nice bend right in the middle and no way was I going down there. Not with these two.

I put my left turn signal on, but instead of making the turn I whipped a fast U-turn, hit the brakes hard and stopped right in the mouth of the street. "End of the line, guys," I said.

"My lady's got a bad leg," the guy whined. "Can't you take us down the block?"

I pointed the mace at his face. "Get the fuck out of my cab," I shouted.

The guy held up his hands like he was under arrest. "Hey, don't be spraying no mace," he said, and opened the door.

The girl didn't want to go. She was sitting right behind me

and I knew she still wanted to try. I pointed the mace her way.

The boyfriend was the brighter of the pair. "Come on," he said from out on the street. She went reluctantly. Sliding slowly across the seat, her hands down, hidden behind the back of my seat, holding some kind of weapon, I was sure.

I didn't wait for them to close the door. I stepped on the gas the minute her feet hit the pavement and the door shut on its own.

"Fucking stupid," I said to myself as I drove away. "You are so fucking stupid." It was just another test, I decided. If you were stupid enough to let white trash in the cab when they told you they didn't have enough money to pay, you would be stupid enough to talk dirty with them, and then drive down a dark little side street and wait to be robbed. I wondered if the Polack would have fallen for the pair and I realized he'd never have stopped at all.

It was three in the morning when I spotted a guy in a business suit signing out of an office building in the financial district at the far end of LaSalle Street. He waved wearily to the night guard, picked up a briefcase and pushed through the revolving door. When he saw me waiting he lifted his free hand and turned it palm up in question. I waved him over.

His suit was rumpled and his tie had disappeared. He opened the door and dropped the briefcase to the street, then stood there going through his pockets. "I've only got forty-two bucks," he said after a while. "I know it's a little short but can you get me to Barrington for that?"

Barrington was an exclusive suburb way the hell northwest. The last train had gone hours before. "Forty-two." I hesitated a moment, as if I were really thinking it over. "What the hell," I said.

"Thanks." He tossed the briefcase into the back seat and climbed in after it. "Get off at Barrington Road," he said as I started to roll. "You might have to wake me when we get there."

"Must be a lawyer," I said.

"How'd you guess?"

"Only ones work these hours."

"Yeah, it's crazy."

"Great for us."

"One man's poison," he said.

The highway was loaded with drunks heading home. The only sober drivers were behind the wheels of cabs and trucks. There wasn't a cop in sight.

A few minutes out of the Loop, I was in the left lane passing a flatbed truck when a Caddy came barreling up flashing its lights. I glanced in the mirror and my passenger was sitting there wide awake.

"Can't sleep?" I asked.

"Something about this traffic," he said.

"Half of 'em have been drinking since five," I said.

"Let 'em pass," he said. "That's my advice."

I drifted right and the Caddy came shooting through blasting its horn.

"What kind of law you do?" I asked.

"Corporate," he said, "mergers, that sort of thing."

"Sounds pretty interesting," I said.

"Most boring thing in the world. Believe me."

"Why do it?"

He shrugged. "Where the money is."

"You ever do any divorce work?"

"Christ," he said. "That'd be even worse."

"I guess that's what I need," I said. "A divorce lawyer. I mean, I'm already divorced, but I guess if I wanted some advice that's what I should look for."

He didn't say anything. I glanced in the rearview and he was sitting there wide awake. "What's it usually run out to Barring-ton?" he asked a while later, and then answered his own question. "Fifty, fifty-five," he decided.

"Something like that," I agreed.

"And then there's the tip," he said. "So I'm probably shorting you what, about twenty bucks?"

"This time of night, I'm glad to get the forty-two," I told the truth.

"So tell me why you think you need this divorce lawyer?"

"It's a pretty long story," I said.

"You've got me trapped," he said. "You'll never get a lawyer this cheap."

"I don't know where to start."

"Try the beginning."

"See, I used to have a good job." I tried to explain how my life had come apart. "I didn't always do this."

"Okay," he said.

"And then I got fired and couldn't find anything."

"And your wife decided she wanted out."

"How'd you guess?"

"It's pretty classic."

"Really?" I don't know why this made me feel better but it did.

"Oh, sure," he said. "A lot of women, the minute the pay-check disappears they do too."

"I couldn't really blame her," I said. "I was a mess. You know, drinking all night, sleeping all day. So I didn't contest anything. She got the house. She got custody. I got visitation on Sunday afternoons."

"How many kids?"

"Just one," I said. "A girl. She's gonna be sixteen next month."

"How about child support?"

"Well, when we got divorced, I still wasn't working and my unemployment had run out, so there wasn't any."

"Then you got a job."

"Yeah, stupid fucking job, way the hell out in Addison. But it was the only thing I could get. I took home about two hundred a week and the judge decided about half of that should be child support. I did okay for a while, but then there was just no way. I mean, the car breaks down, you got to fix it. So now I couldn't even see my own kid."

"And?"

"My wife kept dragging me into court, trying to get money. They put a lien on my pay but the job didn't last and I was back on unemployment for a while. I got another job, worse than the first. I didn't tell my ex about it, but she found out and put a wage assignment on that check. Anyway, eventually, I owed about six thousand dollars. One day her lawyer came up to me with this agreement. He said if I signed it they'd forget about the child support."

"You have a lawyer look at it?"

"No."

"What did it say?"

"That it was okay for my ex-wife to move out of state and that I couldn't have any contact with my daughter until she turned twenty-one."

"And now you want to see your daughter?"

"It's been seven years."

"It's kind of hard for me to believe that any judge would go along with an agreement that sounds so clearly out of line. Are you sure it was filed with the court?"

"I don't know," I had to admit. "We were in the hallway outside the courtroom."

"Did you go into court after you signed it?"

"I don't think so," I said.

"Well, my guess is that agreement is pretty much worthless. But the first thing to do is have a lawyer take a look at it, and then dig out the court file and see if they filed it. I can recommend someone, if you want."

"I don't have a copy," I said.

"You lost it?"

"I never had it," I explained. "I just signed it and the lawyer took it back."

"You signed a contract and you didn't keep a copy?"

"I guess so," I said.

"Do you know what that means?"

"No," I admitted.

"Well, let's hope they filed it. Otherwise how do you prove it ever existed?"

"I don't get you."

"Say she drags you into court and wants child support for the last seven years."

"That was part of the agreement," I said.

He smiled and held his arms wide. "What agreement?"

"Oh, Jesus," I said.

"Here," he said, "let me give you a guy's name." He wrote on the back of a business card and handed it up. "He's expensive. But mention my name and tell him you're a cabdriver."

"It's okay," I said. "I've got some money in the bank."

"Christ," he said. "Never tell a lawyer that."

On the way back into the city I got off the highway at North Avenue and headed east. There were girls everywhere. They were parading up and down the avenue, jumping in and out of cars, and flashing passing motorists. But the girl I was hoping to see was nowhere around.

I got a late start Saturday night, and then I couldn't find a load.

I did the circuit for a while: Clark to Halsted, Lincoln to Wells, North to Halsted back to Clark, up to Belmont, to Sheffield, to Addison and then back to Halsted. There were empty cabs everywhere, waiting for the smallest crumb to fall their way, fighting for every load, driving like fools.

An American–United came around my right on Lincoln Avenue and jumped the light to beat me off the line. I let him go. He got a load at the next corner. I continued past. At Armitage there were three girls looking for a cab. I waved them across the street but they shook their heads and pointed back the way I'd come.

The early show was breaking at Second City but there was already a long line of empty cabs double-parked in front.

Waiting for the light at Clark and Division, a Flash Cab pulled to my right and his passenger got out. A guy standing on the corner suddenly decided he needed a cab and slid into the Flash's back seat. The Flash turned right on red, and a Yellow took his place and then jumped the light.

I took Maple east and drove around the small park where Rush Street meets State. A skinny guy in a dark suit was standing on a fire hydrant on the edge of the park holding a thick bible in his hand. "Repent?" he shouted over the sounds of Saturday night, and there was clear disbelief in his voice. "Even if you people wanted to repent you couldn't. There's no way you could ever repent. You don't even know all your sins." Nobody seemed to be paying any attention.

I followed an empty Checker past the bars on Division Street. Neither one of us got a load and the cops kept us moving along. The Checker made a right on Wells Street. I slowed down and the light turned red.

A few seconds later a horn sounded behind me. I looked in the mirror. There was an empty Yellow back there. The driver was waving his arms around. I continued to sit there. I wanted to put some space between myself and the Checker. There wasn't much percentage in following empty cabs.

When the light changed, I made a right and then moseyed up the block, the Yellow still trapped behind me. He kept blasting his horn and looking for an opening to pass but there was traffic coming our way.

A few blocks up, a well-dressed guy was standing on the curb looking up at a sign that advertised PEEP SHOW. As I approached he turned towards the street and raised an arm into the air.

I pulled to the side and the Yellow came flying around, horn blaring, the driver waving his arms as he sped past.

The guy opened the back door and leaned into the cab. "There's supposed to be a strip joint around here someplace," he said. He was wearing one of those HELLO MY NAME IS tags. "Bill Harrison," was written in red.

"You're about ten years too late," I let him know.

"No, listen," he said, "another cab just dropped me off. He said there was a place right around here."

I shook my head. "He must have meant that peep show," I

said. "If you're looking for strippers—girls, anyway—the closest place is out in Cicero."

"Cicero," the guy said as if the name rang some bell. "Shit, I'm not going to Cicero."

"I don't blame you," I said. "There's another place up on the Northwest Side, probably about a twelve-dollar ride. The only problem is there's no booze."

"You're shitting me."

I shook my head.

"Man, I thought this was Chicago," the guy said, stretching the name out. "I never heard of a dry strip joint."

"Used to be go-go joints all over this street," I said.

"Girls in cages," he said wistfully.

"That's right," I remembered, "go-go boots and nothing else."

"There any street action around?" he asked softly.

"I don't know nothin' 'bout that," I lied.

"Unbelievable," he shook his head.

"Your best bet is to go back to your hotel and call one of those escort services. They'll come right to your room."

He gave me a suspicious look. "What gives you the idea I'm at a hotel?"

"That tag you're wearing."

He looked down. "Shit," he said. He unpinned the tag and dropped it to the street. "Like wearing a big sign says chump."

"You need a cab?"

"There ain't nowhere to go." He laughed and dropped a dollar bill over the front seat. "Thanks for the line," he said, and he closed the door, turned and headed back towards the peep show.

Up the street a group of people were climbing into the Yellow. I started around and the driver stuck his arm out the window and gave me the one-finger salute.

"Same to you, buddy," I said as I passed. "Same to you."

✿

It was after eleven when a couple of guys stumbled out of a Lincoln Avenue bar. They were both young and white. One guy was husky, wearing a sweatshirt and no jacket. The second guy was on the skinny side. He was so drunk he could barely stand.

"Where to?" I asked.

"God, you're white and you speak English," the not-so-drunk guy said. "That's fucking different."

"Unbelievable," the drunk agreed.

"Where you going?" I tried again.

"Evanston," Not-so-drunk said.

"Well, that narrows it down," I said.

"Alright," the drunk wanted to know, "what about you? What about you?"

Not-so-drunk didn't pay any attention to him. He leaned over the front seat and gave me an address on Asbury Street. "I had my rights read to me, big time," he said as I started away.

"A woman," I guessed.

"You're an inspiration," he said. "You're the first guy all night's been on the same page."

"That's scary," I said, "considering how much you guys have had to drink."

"No, believe me," he said. "I'm not fucked up. He's fucked up." He squinted at my license. "God, your name's Edwin. That's great."

"Eddie," I said.

"I mean, we've seen Hussain. We've seen Nassar. Mohammed."

"Hussain was the last one," the drunk chimed in. "He's from Libya."

"What's been your best fare tonight?" Not-so-drunk asked.

"Money wise, you mean?"

"No, the most interesting."

"Well, somebody threw up a while ago."

"Don't tell us that," he said, and then he dropped back to the seat.

"I think I got most of it," I said.

"What'd he say? What'd he say?" the drunk wanted to know.

Not-so-drunk was back over the seat a minute later. "You seem like a nice guy," he said. "What the hell you doing driving a cab?"

"What's wrong with driving a cab?" I asked.

"I've seen all these other guys," he said.

"Hey, it beats the shit out of pounding the pavement."

"How much you make doing this?" he asked.

"You with the IRS?"

"No, no," he said. "Just wondering."

"Do you own your own cab or do you lease?" The drunk was suddenly coherent.

A few blocks later they were both snoring.

I took Lake Shore until it ended, then Hollywood into Ridge. This was the same route I'd followed the other night, when I'd been playing detective. Now I was doing it the right way, with someone paying for my time.

We passed the 24-Hour Pantry. The parking lot was crowded. A Yellow Cab was just pulling in.

Evanston was one of those suburbs with streetlights left over from Edison's time. I cruised up Asbury for several blocks unable to find a number.

"Hey wake up, guys," I shouted. I turned the inside light on to help them along. "Are we close?"

Not-so-drunk opened his eyes. "Jesus, we're here already," he said. "Just pull over anywhere."

I stopped. "All right guys," I said. "It's twelve-fifty."

"That's it?" the drunk asked.

"Fourteen-fifty," I decided.

"That's better," the drunk agreed.

"How about a tip," Not-so-drunk asked. "What do you want for a tip?"

"Sixteen-fifty," I said. I didn't want to be too greedy.

Not-so-drunk took a look at the meter then handed me a ten, a five, and three singles.

The drunk suddenly bent over. "Hey, don't throw up in here," I shouted, although it would have served me right, after my nasty little joke. "Open the door."

"I dropped something," he muttered.

"There it is, right there," Not-so-drunk said. He reached down, picked up a ten dollar bill and handed it to the drunk.

"I'll tell you what," the drunk said, and he held the bill towards me.

"No. No," Not-so-drunk shouted.

"He already paid me," I tried to explain.

"I'll tell you what, too bad," the drunk said and he handed me the ten. "Thank you."

"What are you, a fucking idiot?" Not-so-drunk wanted to know.

"I'm a nice guy," the drunk said.

Not-so-drunk looked at me. I shrugged. "I'm a cabdriver," I said. "I take all the money people give me."

"Fucking idiot," Not-so-drunk said, and he pushed the drunk right out of the cab. "Best ride you had all night, I'll bet," he said as he crawled out behind him.

As I pulled away, they were rolling around on the grass, shouting and laughing, waking up the neighborhood.

When I got to the 24-Hour Pantry the Yellow Cab was gone. I pulled in. All I really wanted was coffee.

Rollie started in on me the minute I walked through the

door. "Shit, here he come again," he said, and several customers looked my way. "Big fool cabdriver like to go talking to the po-lice."

I held up my hands and headed towards the back. "Hey, I thought we were pals," I said.

"I didn't even know your friend," Rollie said, as he followed along behind the deli case. He went on and on as I poured my coffee. "You the fool. You know that? You don't know nothing 'bout nothing but there you go talking to the police. You best be careful, you start steppin' in my shit."

"Look," I tried again as I started for the front. "I thought we went through this last night."

"And you can buy your own goddamn coffee, man," he shouted as he followed me back towards the register. There were two people waiting for him, a six-pack and a couple of chicken pot pies lined up on the counter. Mohammed was in his regular spot, his eyes dead ahead.

I walked past the line and dropped a dollar bill on the counter. "Keep the change, Rollie," I said, and headed for the door.

"Man, fuck you and your chump change," he shouted behind me and I heard the register spring to life, and then something hit me in the back as I was going out the door.

The coins fell to the pavement and scattered around the parking lot. Where was the panhandler tonight, I wondered, with money just waiting there on the ground?

I hadn't driven a block before a familiar looking guy leaning against a parked Checker waved. I pulled to the side. He grabbed a beaded seat cushion off the Checker's hood.

"Giving it up, huh?" I said as he slid in.

"Yeah, man," he said, and I realized he was another of that rare breed, an American-born driver. "I don't like working too late."

"Don't blame you. Where to?"

"Mohawk and North," he said.

That was Old Town. "Get me back in the action," I said.

"Take Ridge to Ashland," he said, sounding just as obnoxious as a regular passenger. "Ashland to Clybourn. Clybourn to…"

I joined in: "Clybourn to North. North to Mohawk and drop you right on the corner."

"You know your way around," he said.

"Yeah, well, I used to drive a cab back in the old days," I said.

He grinned, but I could tell he'd missed the point.

"Hey, what's your name, guy?" he asked as we waited for the light at Peterson.

"Eddie," I said.

"Nice to meet you, Eddie," he said. "I'm Billy."

"How you doing, Billy?"

"Can't complain," he said. "Goin' to see my lady."

"Sounds like fun," I said.

I followed Ridge to Clark and then went south on Ashland. The drunks were heading north, passing and weaving, running without lights or with their brights blazing away. I flashed my own brights a couple of times but nobody paid any attention.

"You been making any money out here?" Billy asked.

"It's been pretty good," I said. "I just had a couple of guys give me twenty-eight bucks for a fourteen dollar load."

"That's good, man."

"You gotta get lucky occasionally," I said. "How about you?"

"I do okay," he said. "Did you hear about that Polish guy?"

"Lenny," I said.

"I hear a lot of guys are getting guns."

"I've been thinking about it myself," I admitted.

"Ain't got one yet, huh?"

I held up the can of mace. "Just this," I said. "How about you?"

"I got a rod," he said softly.

"Really?"

"I ain't taking no chances," he said. Then he leaned over the back of my seat and showed me a small, blue-steel automatic. "What do you think?"

"Yeah," I said. "That's what I need. Something not too big. What's that, a .22?"

".32, man. Take some asshole's head right off, you have to."

"Ain't it a bitch," I said. "You gotta go to work with a gun to make a living in this fuckin' town."

"I been telling people how hard cabdrivers work," he said as he sat back. "Most people they work their five days. But you know, being a cabdriver, you work every day, right?"

"That's about it," I agreed. "What kind of shift you pulling?"

"I do nights."

"Yeah, I figured that much," I said. "What hours?"

"Four to midnight," he said. "See, I just quit. Got off a little early tonight."

"An eight hour shift? That's nice." It was almost unheard of, in fact. "What kind of nut you paying?"

"Huh?"

"How much you pay for the cab?"

"Seventy-seven," he said.

"Seventy-seven dollars for eight hours?" That's what some companies charged for a 24-hour cab. It was much more than I paid for twelve.

"I make out okay," he said.

"Really?" I said. He was either a liar or someone was playing him for a sucker. And then, just like that, it came to me who he really was. Suddenly, I knew why he looked so familiar. And I realized how easily Lenny and I had been conned, how easily everybody had been conned.

I could suddenly see Billy up along Ridge the other night

standing alongside a parked cab. He'd drawn a circle in the air as I'd passed and I thought he was trying to tell me it was a nothing night. Now, I realized what he'd really wanted was a ride. He was asking me to circle back after I dropped my passenger.

But Lenny, a minute or two behind me, had shown up instead.

"What we need is more rain," Billy said.

"I hate driving in the rain," I said mechanically.

"Yeah, but the money's good," he said, driving another nail into my coffin.

It was the day drivers who prayed for rain, sleet, and snow. Night drivers generally preferred good weather. At night, bad weather usually kept everybody close to home.

I slowed down a bit. What was the hurry?

If I ever got the chance, I would have to apologize to Rollie. It would be my turn to buy the coffee. Fuck, I'd buy the whole goddamn store.

"Something wrong, Eddie?" Billy asked after a while.

"Just tired," I said.

"What you need is some rest. You probably been working too hard."

"Probably," I agreed.

This far north, Ashland was a wide, residential street. There was plenty of traffic but there wasn't a cop in sight.

I slipped the mace out of the ashtray and set it on my lap. Maybe I could turn around like the old black driver in the detective's story and just spray away. Yeah, sure. My new friend Billy probably had the gun in his hand. I didn't stand a chance.

I was scaring myself silly, I decided a few blocks later. He probably was just another in a long line of dumb-as-a-box-of-rocks cabdrivers who didn't know a damn thing about their own business. Being on Ridge the other night didn't necessarily make him a murderer. I decided to give him another chance. "Your owner live up by Devon?" I asked.

"My what?"

"Your owner," I said again. "You drive for a private owner, right?"

"I drive for Yellow," he said.

"Oh," I said. He'd been leaning against a Checker, most of which were privately owned. But maybe he'd parked the Yellow across the street or around the corner somewhere. "You must have a foreign dayman," I tried again.

"Why you keep asking all these questions, man?"

"Just making conversation," I said.

"See, I've only been doing this for a couple of months," he said. "So I don't really know all the lingo."

"Just do it when you need money, huh?"

He thought that was funny. "That's right," he said, and chuckled for a while. "That's exactly right. You're too smart to be driving a cab, Eddie. You know that?"

"Yeah," I said. "That's me, all right." I'd been telling myself the same thing for years and now here was somebody who finally agreed.

We were coming up to the six-corner intersection of Lincoln, Belmont and Ashland. Once upon a time this had been the biggest shopping district on the North Side. Now all the department stores were gone. Many of the buildings were completely deserted. Huge FOR SALE and FOR RENT signs were everywhere.

One thing remained from the old days. The intersection was NO LEFT TURN 24 hours a day. And usually there was a squad car hiding somewhere, trying to make the monthly quota off some stray motorist.

I timed it so Billy wouldn't have a chance to stop me. I slowed to let a couple of cars clear then I jumped on the gas and turned left just in front of a CTA bus moseying north in the right lane.

"Where you going, man?" Billy shot up and leaned over the front seat.

"This is a little shorter," I said, which was true. "Lincoln to Larrabee to North, save you some money." No blue lights appeared in my mirror which didn't really surprise me. They were never around when you wanted them.

"No. No. No," Billy said. "Take the next right."

I was doing about forty-five, a nice even twenty over the limit, and I didn't slow down.

"Where the fuck you going?" he shouted as we passed through the intersection. Something cold and hard touched the nape of my neck, and a hand grabbed my hair and snapped my head back.

"Slow down, motherfucker," he said as the steel dug into my skin.

I slowed down. "You ain't no cabdriver," I said evenly.

"Now you're gonna make the next right or I'm gonna blow your fucking head off. Understand?"

"Yeah," I managed to say.

I put the right turn signal on. The Golden Batter Pancake House was a half a block ahead on the left. There wasn't a cab in sight. But a squad car was parked in the bus stop.

"Keep your cool, Eddie. You'll be okay," Billy whispered. He released my hair. "Ain't nothin' bad gonna happen, Eddie. You gotta trust me now. Just keep your cool. Keep your cool."

And I could hear him saying those same words to Lenny. "Ain't nothing bad gonna happen, Lenny." And I saw that picture of Lenny again, one dead eye surrounded by slaughter.

I started into the turn and then ducked and laid on the brakes as hard as I could. He came halfway over the front seat and I threw an arm at him and jumped on the gas and cut the wheel hard left. He went flying backwards but I didn't give him a chance to rest. I braked hard again, and this time when he came hurtling forward I got him square in the head with my forearm. The gun went off twice—close and loud—and before I could get my foot back on the gas we bounced over a safety island and the gun sailed out of his hand, slid along the front seat and fell to the floor. I grabbed the mace with one hand, the steering wheel with the other, laid on the brakes and sprayed away.

We came to a stop with the front of the cab on the sidewalk. Billy-boy had his hands to his face. I gave him a few more squirts, just to be sure, but then I began to feel the mace myself. I reached down and grabbed the gun and jumped out of the cab. Billy-boy was coughing away back there, trying to open the door. I ran around the car and opened it for him and he crawled out coughing, his hands to his face.

I slapped him with the gun a few times. I was yelling something about Lenny, I don't remember what. The shots were still ringing in my ears. Billy-boy dropped his hands and his face was covered with blood.

I gave him one final slap and then decided he'd had enough. I grabbed him by the neck and pushed him towards the restaurant.

A pair of uniformed cops met us at the door. "This is the guy..." I said, and that was as far as I got.

One cop grabbed me and slammed me against the wall of the restaurant, pulling the gun out of my hand and pinning my arms behind my back. The other cop slipped handcuffs on my wrists and started to push me towards the squad car.

"Hey, he's the guy you want," I shouted. "He's the guy…"

"Save your energy, pal," the cop said, squeezing the handcuffs tight. "You're gonna need it where you're heading."

"He went crazy on me." Billy-boy figured out which way the wind was blowing. "I don't know what happened." He coughed. "Next thing I know, he pulled a gun."

"This guy…" I tried again but the cop threw me against the squad and began to frisk me.

Billy-boy coughed. "Then he starts spraying mace," he said. "Fucking dude is crazy."

"You just sit still," the other cop said, "we'll get you an ambulance."

"This guy…" I tried one last time.

The first cop opened the door of the squad car and shoved my head down. Clair came running up, still dressed in street clothes. "Eddie, are you okay?" she called as they pushed me into the back seat.

"Call Detective Hagarty over at Belmont and Western," I managed to shout. "Tell him it's the guy. It's the guy." I tried to point my head towards Billy.

He'd gotten a towel from someone. He was wiping the blood from his face but I swear he winked as the cops slammed the door and locked me inside the cage.

"It's the guy," I shouted as loud as I could.

Upon being given a destination by a passenger, the public chauffeur shall proceed immediately to such destination by the most direct route, unless directed by the passenger to take another route.

City of Chicago, Department of Consumer Services,
Public Vehicle Operations Division

"Look, you got the wrong guy," I said as we pulled away from the pancake house, leaving the flashing lights of the ambulance behind.

"Shut it," the cop behind the wheel said.

"Or we'll shut it for you," his partner said. He banged my cage with his nightstick.

I had no better luck with the cops at the station house. They weren't calling any detectives for me. This was the same station I'd visited the other night.

Before long, I found myself sitting on the floor in the back of a crowded lockup. I was between a Mexican kid, in for drunk driving, and an older black guy, on his way home to the penitentiary.

"I was just out for a little vacation," the black guy explained without sorrow. "I like to come out every couple years, make sure the world's still round. But six month's about all I can stand. These streets will kill you, you hang around too long."

My only hope was that Clair had understood my frantic shouting. But would Hagarty and Foster understand what she meant? Would they get my message before Billy-boy up and disappeared?

I closed my eyes and listened as the Mexican told his story. He'd been tooling along Kedzie Avenue earlier in the evening when he'd dropped a lit cigarette. He'd reached down to pick it up and the next thing he knew he was sitting right in the middle of a 7-Eleven, the wheels on his car still spinning, plastic eggs loaded with pantyhose bouncing all over the hood.

"I'm trying to get the thing in reverse and this chick reaches in and jerks the key right out. You believe that shit?" the kid asked. "Bitch didn't even work there. Then she runs out the store and hides till the cops show up. Fuckin' people ought to mind their own fuckin' business, man."

"Just another reason not to smoke," the black guy let him know.

"The fucking idiot cops," I said. "They see me beating the shit out of the guy and that's it. I'm the bad guy. Not a brain between the two of 'em. Christ, they wouldn't listen to a word I said."

"That's right," the Mexican chimed in, "they don't hear a thing. I told 'em I just stopped in to get a six-pack but…"

"My man, you are exactly right," the black guy agreed. "Exactly. The cop asks me what I'm doing in that apartment. 'I'm looking for my dog,' I say. 'What's this dog's name?' cop wants to know. 'Josephine,' I tell him.

" 'Josephine,' he starts calling. 'Here, Josephine. Here, Josephine.' He turns to me, 'No Josephine here.'

" 'Hell, I know that,' I say. 'What would she be doing here? She's waiting for me back at Vandalia.' " He chuckled softly.

Normally I might have laughed, too. But I wasn't in a laughing mood. How many cabdrivers had Billy-boy killed, and how many more would he have a shot at now that they'd let him go?

I heard someone shouting out in the hallway. "Miles," the voice called. "Edwin Miles."

I stood up.

"That you?" the black guy said.

"It's me," I said warily, and I worked my way towards the front of the cell.

"Miles," the voice shouted again. "Edwin Miles."

The turnkey was standing there with a sheet of paper in his hand. Hagarty and Foster were right behind him.

"I'm Eddie Miles," I said.

"This your guy?" the turnkey asked.

"That's our hero," Hagarty said.

The turnkey unlocked the cell. "Alright Mr. Miles," he said, "time to go."

"Come on, jailbird," Hagarty said, and he grinned from ear to ear.

I just stood there. "What's so goddamn funny?" I asked.

"A can of mace against an automatic," Foster said, "you don't think that's funny?"

Somebody pushed me from behind. "Come on, man," a voice said. "You're out. Get the fuck out."

"You're already a legend," Hagarty said as I stumbled into the hallway.

"But they let him go," I said.

"Relax," Hagarty said, "he's sitting upstairs."

"You got him?"

Hagarty nodded.

"They wouldn't listen to me," I said.

"What you get for interrupting policemen when they're eating," Foster told me. "Why didn't you just bring him straight here and skip that whole pancake house routine?"

I followed them out to the parking lot.

"I'll bet money he's the guy killed Lenny," I said.

"No need, he already confessed," Hagarty let me know. "Plus that guy on Goethe." He pronounced it *go-thee*. "And another guy from about a year and a half ago, and two guys in Vegas."

"Vegas?" I said.

"That's where he started," Hagarty said. "He busted out at the crap tables one night and the only way he could think to get back in the game was to take out a cab."

"Had the guy drive him out to the desert and popped him," Foster said.

"Only problem was, an hour later he's broke again," Hagarty went on. "But the next cab was the charm. He put a little streak together and made it home a winner. From then on, every time things got a little tight, he'd go find himself a taxicab."

Hagarty unlocked an unmarked car and held the rear door for me. "Where we going?" I asked.

"Thought we'd give you a ride back to your cab," Hagarty said. "Maybe buy you a cup of coffee, ask a couple of questions. It's crowded as hell upstairs."

"The weekend rush," Foster said as Hagarty pulled away.

Nobody said anything for a while. I looked in all the store windows we passed, something I seldom had a chance to do.

"I'll tell you," I said after a while, "when I saw him get in that ambulance, I thought he was gone for good."

"Guy's so dumb," Foster said. "He was sitting in the emergency room waiting his turn with all the other losers."

"He's got this little bump on his nose," Hagarty laughed, "but Billy's convinced it's broken and he's not going anywhere till he sees a doctor."

"That's really his name?" I asked.

"William Lincoln Calloway," Foster said.

"Why would he give me his real name?"

"You weren't gonna be around to tell anybody," Foster said.

Somebody had straightened out my cab. It was still blocking the crosswalk but it was off the sidewalk. Hagarty made a U-turn and pulled up behind it. Foster opened the door so I could get out. I walked up and pulled a parking ticket off the windshield.

"We'll take care of that," Hagarty said. He pulled it out of my hand and handed it to Foster, who dropped it into a file folder.

I tried the door but it was locked.

"I got 'em," Foster said. He searched through the folder for a moment then handed me the keys.

"Evidence guys had to tear the seat up a little," Hagarty said, but the interior of the cab wasn't too bad. There was some blood on a back window. The bullets had gone into the front seat over on the passenger side. The holes had been enlarged and some of the stuffing pulled out. It was nothing that a little duct tape wouldn't cure. But I could already hear Irv whining.

Billy's beaded seat cushion was sitting on the dashboard, still rolled and tied with a string. "This is his," I said as I pulled it out.

"Keep it as a souvenir," Hagarty said.

I shook my head. "I'd always be wondering where he got it."

Foster took it, locked it in the trunk of their car, then we all walked inside. It was a quarter to three and the place was starting to fill with the early bar rush.

Clair gave me a big hug. "You okay, Eddie?"

"I'm great," I said. "Thanks for getting these guys."

Ken Willis, Ace, Fat Wally and the rookie were at the roundtable. I waved and motioned that I would be over in a while. Fat Wally started to applaud. After a moment Ace and Willis stood up and joined in. The rookie beamed. I took a little bow before settling into a side table. The drunks didn't know what the hell was going on.

"My fans," I said as I sat down.

"Hey, you deserve it," Hagarty said. "Took balls."

"I kept seeing that picture of Lenny," I remembered.

"Now if Billy was a better shot," Foster said, "we'd be down at the morgue right now going through your pockets, talking about what a fool you'd been."

"What's going to happen to him?" I asked.

"Firing squad, we're hoping," Foster said. "Maybe a hanging."

"Something barbaric," Hagarty said. "You can't go killing stagecoach drivers out West. He'd probably get life here, and even if the judge did decide to zap him, it'd take years. But we figure Nevada's gonna pull his chain. They got two guys on the way right now, including a Lieutenant." Suddenly he sounded like John Wayne. "They don't take too kindly to folks messing with their citizens out thataway."

Clair poured coffee all around. Foster ordered a piece of cherry pie. Hagarty lit a cigarette.

"It's kind of funny it was a white guy," I said after the pie arrived.

Hagarty shrugged. "Your friend's just as dead."

"I know," I said. "But here you've got every cabdriver in town passing up black passengers and staying out of certain neighborhoods. It's just kind of funny."

Hagarty shrugged again. "I wouldn't get too careless, I was you."

Foster was working his way through the pie. He mumbled in agreement.

"You ever find that van?" I asked.

Hagarty shook his head and smiled. "The shit you put us through," he said.

"What?" I asked.

"The guy goes dumpster diving at Fulton Market," he said. "That's why he kept driving by that whore."

"Dumpster diving?" I asked.

"Spoiled meat. Meat scraps," Hagarty said. "Whatever the packing houses dump. He's got a little route. We were afraid to ask where he sells the stuff."

"You should have seen the back of that van," Foster said.

"Evidence guys are never gonna forgive us."

"And while we were wading through that shit," Foster said, "the real guy was down in Peoria doing another whore."

"Peoria?"

"He's finally snapped," Foster said. "It's just a matter of time now."

"Three girls in a week," Hagarty shook his head.

"Way out of his cycle," Foster said.

"Three?" I asked.

Hagarty nodded. "Where's that picture?"

Foster started digging around in his file folder. "Here," he said after a moment, and he slid an eight-by-ten across the tabletop.

"Ever see her before?" Hagarty asked.

"Oh, Jesus," I said. It was a picture of a young black girl. There was no expression on her face, but the pigtails and a lonely blue ribbon let me know who she was. There was nothing at all behind those eyes.

"Yes?" Hagarty asked. Foster had his notebook open, pen in hand.

"The other night," I whispered, and I pushed the picture away.

"You're sure it's her?" Hagarty asked.

I nodded my head. "When did you…When did you…You know."

They knew. "A couple hours after you called," Hagarty said. "Factory out on Goose Island. Truck driver found her in a loading dock."

"Did he…" I started but then I couldn't finish. I dropped my head into my hands.

After a while I lifted my head and everything was still the same. There were the cops and the cabdrivers, and the drunks heading home from their Saturday night.

Across the street there was an old stone church with a big cross set on a high steeple. It must have really been something when they'd set that cross in place. I wondered how many men it had taken. There must have been a big crowd down below. I wondered if they'd all truly believed, if they'd all really been saved.

Clair came by and topped the coffees. "Just for the record," Foster said and he held the photo up, "you're telling us this is the girl you saw getting into a van early Friday morning?"

"I didn't see her get in," I said. "She was just leaning in the window."

"But this is the girl you saw?"

I nodded my head.

"Good," they both agreed. Foster slipped the photograph back into the folder.

Hagarty waved Clair over and asked for a check.

"On the house," she said.

"Christ, it's like being back in patrol." Foster smiled.

"What was her name?" I asked after Clair had gone.

"Who?" Hagarty asked.

I pointed to the file folder.

"Oh, Christ, it's another one of those goofball names," he said, and he spelled it out. "Y-o-l-a-n-i-c-a, last name Robinson."

"Did you hear about the lady who wanted to name her baby Latrine?" Foster asked.

"Come on," Hagarty said.

"Swear to god," Foster said. "Nurse I know told me about it. They had a hell of a time talking her out of it."

"Hello," Hagarty said. "I want you to meet my daughter Latrine and these are my sons Privy and John."

"You know how Chinese people name their kids?" Foster asked.

"I may have heard this," Hagarty said.

"As soon as the baby's born," Foster explained, "the father runs into the kitchen and dumps the silverware drawer on the floor. Whatever it sounds like, that's the kid's name."

"Anybody ever tell you guys you're a couple of assholes?" I asked.

"All the time," Foster said. "All the fucking time."

Hagarty leaned across the table and let me smell his coffee- and cigarette-scented breath. "She was nothing but a whore," he said in a harsh whisper, and heads turned at the table behind him. "And she wasn't going to be around very long, no matter what you did. Streetwalkers have a very limited life expectancy."

"You keep getting in cars with strange men," Foster added, "bad things are bound to happen."

"Just forget you ever saw her," Hagarty suggested as he pushed his chair back.

They both stood up and then each dropped a buck on the table.

"Take care of yourself, Eddie," Hagarty said.

"See you around," Foster said.

The roundtable had filled up. They were all jabbering away. Clair sat down next to me and put her hand on my shoulder. "You must be tired."

"I don't know," I said.

"You're so tense, Eddie," she said. "I can feel it right here."

She rubbed my shoulder with one hand for a while then brought her other hand up too.

"Don't stop," I said. "Whatever you do, don't stop." I had my head down, my eyes closed. If she would just keep going maybe it would all go away. Maybe I could forget that I'd let a teenage girl die.

"Eddie?" Clair asked after a while.

"Yeah?"

"Do you have a lady friend somewhere?"

"Sort of," I admitted.

"I figured you would," she said with some amusement, and she rubbed a little harder.

"Oh, like that," I said. "Just like that."

"Because that's what you need," she said. "I can do this all night but what you really need is a woman and a warm bed."

"You ever tried getting laid at four in the morning?"

"I usually wait till nine," she said. That was the time she got home, I knew. She was married with kids.

"I'll be back," she said a minute later. "Your pals want coffee."

"Hey, hero," Alex shouted from the roundtable, "you gonna sit there all by yourself?"

"You too good for us now?" Fat Wally wanted to know.

So I went over and sat down and told the story as best I could. My heart wasn't in it but nobody seemed to notice. They cheered and laughed and swore at the two dumb cops, and then they got into some stories of their own.

After a while Ace moved over next to me. "You look about dead," he said as the stories went on.

I held out my hands. I could barely keep them from shaking. "I'm wired is all," I explained.

"You should take a little vacation," he said. "Go lie on a beach somewhere, listen to the waves."

"Maybe I will," I said. "Maybe I will."

"Get the fuck out of the business," he whispered. "That's what you should really do. Go find yourself a decent job."

I shrugged. "A job's a job."

"No," he said and he shook his head. "You know what I keep thinking? Years ago when they tried to pull my license, I should have let 'em."

"They tried to pull your license?" I was surprised. This was one story I'd never heard.

"Oh, sure," he said. "I was a real bandit when I was a kid. Christ, I was a heartless bastard. I used to work the train stations and the bus depots. The shit-kickers would get in the cab with shopping bags for suitcases and hand me a piece of paper with some address on it. I'd look at it. If it was on the South Side I'd say 'Oh, that's in South Chicago, right?' and nine times out of ten they'd fall for it. 'Yeah, that's right,' they'd say because their relatives told 'em they lived on the South Side of Chicago and the shit-kickers didn't know any better. So I'd get the rate book out and I'd turn to the suburban pages and show 'em the rate for South Chicago and usually I got the suburban rate. That's one of the reasons this is such a great bandit town. You got a South Chicago, a North Chicago, an East Chicago and a West Chicago.

"But I got in my share of trouble too. And then this one time they were really going after me. So I got a lawyer that somebody knew, a fixer, and he paid off the commissioner or someone. Cost me three hundred dollars, a small fortune back then. But I got to keep my license.

"Now, hardly a day goes by when I don't wonder what would have happened if I'd just let 'em take the fucking thing. Maybe I would have done something with my life."

"Come on, Ace," I said, "you did a lot."

"What?"

"You got married. You raised your kids. You own your own house."

"I been driving around in circles for forty-three years," he said. "That's what I did."

"Ace, I never heard you talk like this."

"Oh, hell," he said. "I ain't complaining. I made my own decisions. I had a lot of good times. I paid my bills. But it's a shit job, always has been, always will. You're still young, Eddie. You still got time to get out. I mean, do you wanna die 'cause some asshole can't shoot craps?"

He stood up and dropped some money on the table. "Fuck this," he said. "I'm gonna check in." Ace didn't like the late-night crazies. He usually quit early on weekends.

I hung around a few minutes longer, then dropped a pile of singles on the table and waved to Clair.

She caught me by the door. "Eddie," she said, and she gave me the nicest hug I'd had in years. "You're a real live hero," she whispered, and I could feel the warmth of her breath. "Now go find your lady and stay in bed as long as you can."

"Me and you," I said, hugging back. God, she was something.

"That'll be the day." She smiled and pushed me out the door.

I spent a few minutes cleaning up the cab then headed west, into the countryside.

All I wanted to do was drive, get out on the highway, with the middle-of-the-night trucks blazing through town and just follow along and see where they go. Drive until the buildings gave way to farms and fields. Until the sun came up and I was somewhere, anywhere, where it could cross the entire sky and set with barely a shadow.

I wanted to drive until the last drop of gas was gone, until I was so tired that I could pull over, right there on the shoulder of the highway, and fall asleep curled up on the front seat, to wake fully rested in a place I'd never been.

I passed the old Stewart–Warner factory, their original plant, red brick with white trim—lord knows how old—now closed and FOR SALE. ONE MILLION SQUARE FEET, the sign read, 11 ACRES — WILL DIVIDE. And all the jobs gone south or to Mexico, or who-the-hell-knows. And a whole batch of soon-to-be cabdrivers sprinkled around the city waiting for their unemployment to run out. They wouldn't find any union manufacturing jobs, that much was certain.

And someday, some developer would come along and convert their old workplace into trendy lofts, or tear it down completely and build highrises or single-family townhouses especially designed for transplanted suburbanites. The mayor would stop by and say what a great thing it was for the city, and he'd break a bottle of champagne or turn a shovel full of dirt. And the lakefront would expand a little further west, and the cabs would follow along, going where the business was.

And the rest of the city, this huge, incredible city, so many times bigger than the lakefront neighborhoods where I now spent most of my nights; the city where I was born and raised, married and divorced; the city where I had forsaken my own daughter, my only flesh and blood; that city, so sad and true, so real, that city would fall even further behind.

I continued west past the Lathrop Homes, once the pride of Chicago housing projects. There were low-rises and townhouses on the banks of the river, and it wasn't very scary-looking as far as housing projects went. But I never went in there without locking my doors and double-checking to make sure the mace was handy.

There were two guys in Chicago Bulls jackets standing

around a bus shelter smoking cigarettes and trying to look tough. They looked more like kids than men. And maybe they were just a couple of basketball fans who'd snuck out after their mammas had fallen asleep. But maybe they were gangbangers with guns hidden beneath the jackets. I was too old and too white to tell the difference.

One of them flagged me, then smiled so I'd know he was just fooling around. He knew I'd never stop. I waved as I passed, and went over the river. When I came to the expressway I continued straight. It looked like I wasn't going to follow those trucks tonight.

There was something peaceful about it. Almost all the stores were closed out this way. Just driving along with no destination in mind, not really looking for a fare.

Diversey wasn't much to look at, tacky storefronts alongside shabby two-flats. FORTUNES TOLD, a sign proclaimed, PALMS READ. A saloon advertised LOTTO, another promised CERVEZA FRIA.

It wasn't the worst neighborhood in town, but it wasn't an area that cabs generally cruised, and just about everybody had gone home. If someone flagged me, maybe I'd stop, but until then I'd just float along on a river of concrete, under sodium vapor stars.

I caught the light at Pulaski, the beginning of a factory and warehouse zone, and it snapped the spell. I'd made it over three miles without stopping.

When the light changed, I turned left, drove the half mile to Fullerton and turned left again.

Three white clowns were pitching quarters out front of a closed saloon. The area was mostly Puerto Rican and Mexican now. But the sign in front of the bar read WALLY'S TAP. It must have been the last white joint around. And the three guys were probably trying to hold on to a neighborhood they'd loved forever. But eventually they'd give up and move further west or out to the suburbs. And then this would be their old neighborhood for life.

It was a city full of old neighborhoods. A city where nobody stayed anywhere for long.

Straight ahead was the first hint of dawn. Betty would be ready for breakfast soon.

At Southport Avenue, a tall blonde waved. What the hell, I decided, and pulled to the side.

"I'm picking up a friend," she said, leaning over the front seat, pointing the way. She wore a black leather jacket over a flimsy western-style blouse.

I turned the corner, started the meter, then put the car in park in front of a two-flat. A party was ending. There was a circle of people milling about on the sidewalk.

"My friend should be right out," she said. She opened the back door but she didn't get out. I half turned in the seat. She was leaning back, eyes closed, one foot dangling out the open door. The dome light shone softly on her face. Her skin was pale and tinged with red. Her hair was dyed. Dark roots had started to show.

She opened her eyes and caught me watching. "Rough night?" She held my gaze for a long moment. Her eyes were a faded grey, speckled with dark green. Her cheeks were slightly sunken, her nose long and delicate.

"A little crazy," I agreed.

"Must be a tough way to make a living," she decided.

"Sometimes," I said. "How about you? How was your night?"

"Too much dancing," she said.

"Where you guys going?" I asked.

She sat up and then leaned over the front seat. "I'm not

really sure," she said. "What do you think? Where should I go?"

"Somewhere far away," I suggested.

She smiled but didn't say anything. Her breathing had slowed down a bit.

"You smell nice," I said.

"That's probably the gin," she said. "When I was a little girl, I thought gin smelled like Christmas trees, a forest full of Christmas trees." She cupped her hands and blew into them, then sniffed the air. "So what do you think? Do I go home with him or what?"

I shrugged. I was a guy. I'd go home with anybody.

"See, it's our first date," she explained. "Well second, really. It depends how you count."

"One, two, three," I showed her.

She smiled and shook her head. "He's just one of those guys always gets what he wants. You'll see."

"Maybe he can give me lessons."

"I hate to be another in the long parade," she said. "But why am I here?"

The guy showed up a minute later. Another black leather jacket, his blond hair tied in a tight little ponytail.

"Sorry it took so long," he said to the girl as he slid in. Then he gave me an address; a highrise a few blocks south of the financial district. "Do you know how to get there?"

"No problem," I said. I headed to Clybourn then turned southeast.

A few minutes later, the guy asked, "Have you ever had your bare bottom spanked in the back seat of a taxicab?" He didn't bother to lower his voice.

The girl giggled and whispered something I couldn't hear.

"I suppose that means a blow job is out of the question," the guy said in that same loud tone.

A mile down we passed the rickety bench promising salvation. "Yolanica," I said under my breath, and I realized that when I'd had my dream, she was already dead.

I turned on Halsted and we went past Cabrini, under the Ogden Avenue Bridge and over the canal and the river. And then a faint but steady beat drifted up from the back seat, and out of the corner of my eye I could detect some pale object going up and down back there. Was that his hand? Was she really having her bare butt spanked in the back of my cab?

I'd have to buy one of those big mirrors, like the one Ken Willis had, which offered a panoramic view of the back seat. But if I really wanted to stop them, all I had to do was turn around and watch. That usually did the trick with all but the worst of perverts. But for some reason I couldn't turn my head.

The beat continued as I headed south.

At Lake Street I turned left and ran under the el and then down the ramp to the left lane of the highway. I had a half mile to make it over three lanes to the exit for eastbound Congress. There was a line of over-the-road trucks barreling through town in the middle lane.

Some night, I really would follow along.

I took the first lane, then sped up and jumped into the line. An air horn sounded behind me and I looked back. She was giving him head. Her blond hair bounced up and down in his lap, in a slow and steady cadence. And suddenly the whole cab smelled of leather.

The air horn continued to sound and the truck began flashing its brights.

I let a couple of cars pass, then looked back again to take the final lane. She was all the way down now. The guy had both his hands planted firmly on her head, holding her in place. But he wasn't paying any attention to the trucks, or to the air horn still sounding, or the flashing lights, or to the girl in his lap. He was looking straight into my eyes.

I drifted over one more lane and then up the ramp for the Loop. The expressway went right through the main post office, one of the city's many wonders, then ended just over the river. I made a right at the first light.

"We're almost there," I warned them as we passed an old factory that had been converted to lofts.

The girl opened the door the instant the cab stopped rolling and she never looked back on her way to the revolving door. Her backside was as shapely as I'd imagined while listening to that gentle beat.

The guy pulled out a fat roll, found a ten and a five and handed them over. "Thanks for the professionalism," he said, and I had a hard time meeting his eyes.

"Sure," I said, then waited until the door was closing. "Thanks for the show."

He did a little dance on the way into the lobby, lifting his arms above his head, snapping his fingers.

The girl was in there, waiting by the elevators, running her fingers through her hair.

I followed the highway back through the darkness of the post office and, when I came out the other side, the gleaming towers of St. Lucy's, a mile or so west, were almost blinding in the morning sunlight.

I continued on, past the exit for home, and as I got closer I searched for Relita's window; for that little black spot that I knew was there, hidden inside all that reflected sunlight, all that shiny glass and steel. But it was impossible to find.

The hospital lobby was quiet. The reception desk was empty. A sign read: VISITING HOURS 11 A.M.–7 P.M.

I headed for the elevators and no one tried to stop me.

Upstairs, I could hear the laughter from a few doors down, a tight, hard laughter, and I assumed it was Relita's tough-as-nails roommate. But when I stuck my head in the doorway, the roommate was nowhere around.

Relita and another girl were sitting on Relita's bed.

Relita had her legs crossed, her elbows resting on her knees. Both girls were rocking back and forth, talking and laughing. It was amazing what a few days of rest and some hospital food could do. Relita was like a different person. One who was sure to survive, at least for a while.

When she saw me she smiled and waved me over. "Eddie, my man," she said. "This be Sharon."

"Hey," I said, but Sharon didn't say anything in return. She watched with glassy, bloodshot eyes as I came around the foot of the bed and picked a spot by the window. "How you doing?" I asked Relita.

Relita shrugged her shoulders and nodded her head. "I cool."

The room was too bright in the sunlight. Too light and bright. It had looked better in the rain. And Sharon had probably looked better out on the street strutting her stuff.

She was about Relita's age, another skinny teenage whore. And it was obvious that she'd come straight from the streets. She was sitting on the bed facing Relita wearing a shiny, black vinyl skirt slit up to her waist, and a flimsy halter top.

"You *look* like a cabdriver," she muttered after a while, and I guessed that she was high on something or other.

"I be telling Sharon all about you," Relita explained.

"I get me cabdrivers sometimes," Sharon said. "Most of 'em be perverts." She spit out the last word and laughed.

"Now don't be calling no names," Relita said, but she was all smiles.

"Streets full of perverts," Sharon said, barking the word again, "and they all be out last night."

Relita imitated the howl of an animal, and they both laughed, rocking back and forth on the bed.

"Be the moon," Sharon said.

"It was crazy in the cab," I said just for something to say.

"We be friends, right?" Relita reached out her hand and I took it.

"Friends," I said. But we didn't hold hands. It was just a quick, awkward, handshake.

"You know what friends be for?" Sharon laughed.

"What's that?" I asked.

"Shut your mouth, girl," Relita said. And the two of them laughed some more.

"I better be getting home," I decided a few minutes later.

"Wait," Relita said, and she reached into the nightstand. "I got something for you. Here." She handed me one of Margaret Gallos' business cards. "I be moving soon but she know where I be. You call that number and she tell you, and you come and see me."

"Where're you going?" I asked.

"It be for vocational training," she said. "So I don't have to walk the streets no more."

This sent Sharon into another fit of giggles. "Girl, you a whore."

"No, you the whore," Relita snapped. "Look how you all prostituted up."

Sharon lifted her skirt and flashed some hot-pink panties.

"And you still be a whore when I'm a computer op-o-ra-tor," Relita said.

"Hey, that's a good job," I said. I mean, you couldn't go wrong with computers, right?

"First I learn keyboard." Relita sounded excited by the idea. "Then they move me to advanced school."

"That's real good," I said.

"Maybe you pick me up from school someday."

"Sure," I said, although I wasn't exactly sure what she had in mind.

"You a cabdriver," Sharon had the answer. "She want a free ride."

"Girl, you be so bad," Relita said.

On the highway heading home I pulled the business card out of my pocket. Gallos was going to have her work cut out for her, I decided. Relita had seemed right at home with Sharon, a couple of whores sitting on a hospital bed.

It was easier for me to imagine Relita working the streets with one tit, giving discount blow jobs, than it was to see her sitting in an office, words and numbers dancing across a computer screen. That was a leap I couldn't quite make. Like me picking her up from school and the two of us going for a malted.

I held the business card out the window and the wind whipped it out of my hand and it sailed away.

Betty must have been watching the street. Her door opened before I was halfway down the hallway. "Eddie, are you okay?"

"I'm fine," I said.

Her hair was down. She was wearing a light summer dress without a slip. A patch of bright sunlight shimmered on the floor behind her. "I thought something happened."

"Just a long trip," I lied, but then I realized it was true. It had been a long trip to nowhere and now here I was, back where I'd started.

"I was really beginning to worry," she said. "I waited breakfast."

This was part of our Sunday ritual. She would fix breakfast while I took a shower, and then we would retire to the bedroom.

But today, I didn't want a shower or food. I led her straight to the bedroom. "Eddie!" she cried, but she followed along.

I closed the door behind us. "Let me ask you something," I said.

"Well I see you're wide awake this morning."

"Have you ever had your bare bottom spanked on a Sunday morning?" I asked, but I didn't wait for an answer. "Do you like that?" I asked after a while.

"It's okay." She didn't sound very excited. "If you like it."

I had to confess, it wasn't doing much for me either. Eventually, we switched to our old, familiar ways.

We drifted along, just going through the motions of love. And then everything faded except for a smiling black kid with blue ribbons on the end of her braids. She unzipped her jacket and opened it slowly to expose tiny, flawless breasts.

"Beautiful dead girl," I heard myself say and we came to a sudden stop.

"Say what?" Betty said, and I opened my eyes and she was staring straight into them.

I couldn't think of anything to say. All I could do was gaze into the glistening darkness of her eyes. Beyond my own dim reflection was a sadness I'd never noticed before. It was as remote, as untouchable as the moon.

"Eddie, are you okay?"

"I'm fine," I managed to say.

"You sure?"

"Sure," I said.

She reached for a cigarette. "You seem different."

"No, baby. Same old me." It was sad but true. I was nobody's angel.

She blew a stream of smoke my way. "What was all that?"

"Huh?"

"What you said before."

"You're my beautiful girl," I said.

She fixed me with that same dark gaze, and I could read the one-word reply ready on her lips. But then her face softened. "What a lovely lie," she whispered, and she dropped the cigarette in an ashtray and pulled me close.

We stayed like that for a long time and then we started up again, a middle-aged couple, pale and overweight, humping away on a beautiful Sunday morning.

The shades were pulled tight against the daylight.

Nobody was going anywhere.

FOR YOUR SAFETY

PLEASE EXIT

ON CURB SIDE

ONLY

The Best of MWA Grand Master
DONALD E. WESTLAKE!

"A book by this guy is cause for happiness."
— STEPHEN KING

Forever and a Death

Based on Westlake's story for a James Bond movie that was never filmed! Millions will die to satisfy one man's hunger for gold—and revenge…

Double Feature

The movie critic and the movie star—how far would they go to keep their secrets buried?

Memory

With his memory damaged after a brutal assault and the police hounding him, actor Paul Cole fights to rebuild his shattered life.

Brothers Keepers

"Thou Shalt Not Steal" is only the first commandment to be broken when the Crispinite monks of New York City try to save their monastery from the wrecking ball.

Help I Am Being Held Prisoner

A gang of convicts plots to use a secret tunnel not to escape from prison but to rob two banks while they have the perfect alibi: they couldn't have done it since they're already behind bars…